FATAL DIAGNOSIS

**This Large Print Book carries the
Seal of Approval of N.A.V.H.**

FATAL DIAGNOSIS

Mary Kittredge

Thorndike Press • Thorndike, Maine

Library of Congress Cataloging in Publication Data:

Kittredge, Mary, 1949-
     Fatal diagnosis / Mary Kittredge.
        p.   cm.
     ISBN 1-56054-112-1 (alk. paper : lg. print)
     1. Large type books. I. Title.
[PS3561.I868F38   1991]   90-27603
813'.54—dc20   CIP

This novel is a work of fiction. All of the events, characters, names, and places depicted in this novel are entirely fictitious or are used fictitiously. No representation that any statement made in this novel is true or that any incident depicted in this novel actually occurred is intended or should be inferred by the reader.

Thorndike Press Large Print edition published in 1991 by arrangement with St. Martin's Press.

Cover design by Tom Odle.

The tree indicium is a trademark of Thorndike Press.

This book is printed on acid-free, high opacity paper.

FATAL DIAGNOSIS

ONE

"This won't hurt a bit," Helene Motavalli told the little girl as she swabbed the small outstretched arm with an alcohol wipe.

"I know," the child replied. "It's OK, I'm not scared."

Turning, Helene readied the plastic syringe and the small glass collection tubes, shielding the child from the sight of them until the final moment. "My, you're a brave one, aren't you?"

The little girl was nine, with big brown eyes behind thick tortoiseshell glasses. She wore a denim jumper, dark green sweater and green cable-stitched knee socks. Her long dark braids were tied with green ribbons, and on her feet were a pair of Buster Brown shoes, the heavy brown old-fashioned kind. Helene hadn't thought they even made Buster Brown shoes anymore.

The youngster crossed her green-stockinged ankles primly. "No, I'm not brave," she said. "But I'm very grown-up. That," she confided, "means acting like you're brave, even when really you're not."

"I see." Helene checked once more to make sure the blood tubes were all sodium-heparinized greentops and that she had a few spares in case one didn't pull enough vacuum. Few things were worse than having the tube fail after you'd already stuck a person, especially a child. Finally, still blocking the girl's line of sight, she heparinized a 21-gauge needle.

Kids could be fine until they got a look at the needle. Then they were apt to scream bloody murder, kicking and thrashing their incredibly strong little bodies around while Mom or Dad tried to hold them.

Hitting that small, fragile vein was no cinch any time, but when it belonged to little Miss or Mister Destructo, then you were talking hematoma: a great big purple-green bruise where you'd had to go in twice or maybe even three times to get a single tubeful. Maybe a good-sized shiner on you, too, if a flying fist or sneaker managed to connect.

Helene turned, syringe in hand. This child didn't have Mom or Dad with her, and if a kid was going to pitch a fit, now was when it happened. Still, there was no sense showing you expected it, so Helene merely steadied the child's arm, placing her left hand under the child's elbow and poising the needle with her right. The big brown eyes widened a fraction, but that was all.

"Ready?" Helene asked. "Can you hold real still?"

Catching her bottom lip between her teeth, the child moved her head gravely up and down. "Uh-huh," she said faintly, but by that time Helene had already snicked the 21-gauge through the skin and into the bluish vein beneath.

"Mmmph," the child said, her chin coming up a little, but otherwise she didn't twitch. Dark red blood fountained into the green-stoppered tube.

"Worst part's done," Helene said. "Now we just fill up a few more." Smoothly she slipped the first tube off the needle and socketed a new one onto it. More of the child's blood spurted.

"You are being just fabulous," Helene told her, dropping the first tube into the wire basket behind her. "Who taught you how to be so brave — I mean, so grown-up?"

The child blinked shyly. "My dad. He says I should practice for when I have my scar fixed. It's pretty big," she added, "and ugly when I wear a bathing suit."

"Oh my. How did that happen?"

The child looked embarrassed. "I tipped a kettle over on myself when I was little. But my dad put ice on me and now he's having me save up my blood so the doctor can give it back when he's making the scar better. That," she finished, "is why I'm used to having needles."

"Your father sounds like a smart man. You know this blood I'm taking now isn't for your operation, though, don't you?"

"Uh-huh." The big brown eyes grew somber. "I might not get to have it even. The judge might say I have to wait." The child's brow furrowed. "Can I ask you a question?"

"Sure." Helene slid the final green-top onto the needle.

"Um, when you test them, do you know which is which?"

"Whose blood in which tubes, you mean?" Helene slipped the rubber tourniquet from the child's arm. "Nope. Well, I know which ones are your tubes," she amended. "That's what I'll be matching the others with. But for the rest, I only have numbers. I won't know whose tubes matched yours until I look the numbers up in the book where the names are written."

The child nodded seriously. "Like a game, sort of. Only not a very fun game."

"No," Helene agreed. "I expect none of this has been much fun for you, has it?"

She dropped the final blood tube into the basket. The child watched as Helene withdrew the needle from her arm, then took the cotton ball she was offered and pressed it to the puncture mark.

"Press hard," Helene told her, and the little girl obeyed, frowning with concentration. Then she looked up, her brown eyes filled with tears.

"Oh, honey, what's wrong? Did I hurt you? I'm sorry."

The child pressed her lips together and shook her head. The green-ribboned braids swung back and forth.

"But," she appealed, "couldn't you just cheat a little bit? Find out which tubes are which and match them up the way I ask you?" She thought a moment. "I could pay you," she offered. "I save most of my allowance."

Helene was shocked. A nice kid like this, one in a million, smart and polite and sweet — offering a bribe. Why did they all have to fight over her this way and put the poor thing through such a circus?

But of course she knew why. If you read the newspaper or watched TV, you could hardly miss finding out. Helene hoped that wasn't how the child learned what these tests were for.

"No, honey," she said, "I'm afraid I couldn't do that. You see, people have to be able to believe in the results of tests like these. They're very important. Even you have to be

11

able to believe in them, so whatever the answer turns out to be you'll know for sure it's the truth."

"I already know the truth." The child's soft pink lip thrust out mutinously. "I know who my mom and dad are, and even if you take out *all* my blood and test it, they'll *still* be my mom and dad."

And to that there didn't seem to be any good answer, so Helene just took back the blood-dotted cotton and tossed it into the wastebasket. The bluish puncture on the child's arm was barely visible.

"Okay, honey, that's it. All done."

The little girl nodded, slid from the chair, and to Helene's surprise held out her hand to be shaken. Her tears had gone, but the small fingers were still damp and chilly with anxiety.

"Thank you for being so nice to me," she said. "It really didn't hurt a bit. And I'm sorry I asked you to do something wrong. I wouldn't want you to get in trouble or anything."

"I know, honey. It's all right, don't worry about it." You poor little thing, Helene added silently.

Taking back her hand, the child tried to smile and nearly managed. "Good-bye," she said.

She went out through the door to the waiting area. She had told her father that she would be all right alone, so he had been waiting for her out there, reading old issues of *The Immunology Review* and *Lab Management Quarterly*.

If in fact he really was her father, which was what Helene was about to discover. Good luck, honey, she thought as the door closed quietly; I hope it all turns out OK for you.

Taking the three green-topped tubes from the wire basket, Helene dropped them in the pocket of her lab coat and walked through the door to the tissue-typing laboratory.

Inside, the lab smelled faintly of burnt gas, formalin, and Cidex sterilizing solution. Overhead fluorescents gave off a bright white light and a barely audible hum. Floor-to-ceiling wooden cupboards and a black Formica counter ran along three sides of the room; a central freestanding bench held a sink with nozzles labeled Gas, Air, O_2 and Vacuum in addition to the usual Hot and Cold.

Beside the sink stood a rack of clean Pyrex flasks, a Bunsen burner with a red rubber hose running to a gas nozzle, and a squat centrifuge that resembled a pressure cooker. Against the fourth wall stood a counter covered by an exhaust hood, for working with fumes or contaminated aerosols.

Half-blocked by the hood was the laboratory's only window, an ancient double-hung affair: spotless on the inside, grimy on the outside, it afforded a narrow view of a small square of sky. On summer days Helene would have liked to open this window, but its lock was frozen and the frame had been painted shut years ago.

Now Helene ignored the window in favor of the thermostat, fiddling with it in hopes of coaxing up some heat. Her attentions produced a small clicking from the mechanism and a series of protesting thumps from the ventilator, but no warm air.

Shrugging, she buttoned her lab coat, under which she wore jeans and sweater, sneakers, and a Timex digital wristwatch that also functioned as a stopwatch, alarm clock, and programmable calculator. As she readied a Hamilton syringe and a set of microtitre plates at the lab bench, the watch read 9:25 A.M.

Turning to her clipboard she began filling in another tissue-typing worksheet, her fifth of the morning. Copying from the labels on the blood tubes, she listed the child's name, date of birth, when the samples had been obtained and by whom, and the child's recent transfusion history. On this line, as on the other four worksheets she had filled out this morning, Helene wrote "None."

To record the chain of custody under which the samples were secured between drawing and testing, she wrote "Does not apply — proc. immed. p̄ venipunct." and initialed this. On the line asking how the client had been identified, she listed "Photo ID #4525667-S, State of Connecticut," thinking as she did so that no nine-year-old girl should have to prove her identity to anyone, much less to some stranger getting ready to stick a needle in her arm.

Then, having completed the appropriate paperwork, she turned her attention to the procedure at hand. It was picky work and time-consuming, but not particularly difficult, first separating red cells from white cells and serum with a specific-gravity solution, then spinning the white cells into a pellet in the centrifuge.

Next, the white cells were tricked into separating further; the T-cells would adhere to a column of nylon wool suspended in fetal calf serum, while the B-cells would not. Then the T-cells were washed off with warm solutions and the B-cells aggregated with cool. Finally the microtitre plates were prepared.

With an auto-pipette calibrated to millionths of a liter, Helene dropped a microliter of T-cell solution into each of the plastic plate's seventy-two small wells. Each well already contained a microliter of antiserum, a different type for each well, so that when the careful task of pipetting was done she had only to cover all the plates with glass slides, set them in the incubator, and wait: an hour for T-cells, three for B-cells.

If her luck ran right she would be finished by five and out of here on time, for once; with organ transplants running at the rate of two a day in the state — a hundred a day nationwide — she'd been busy as hell lately, matching available organs with people who needed new kidneys, livers, lungs, or hearts.

Cold weather slowed things for a time, as motorcycle season ended and the pool of organ donors dried up temporarily. But soon snowmobiling and icy-road accidents would begin, treating the demand for healthy tissue to a renewed supply of harvestable cadavers.

So tonight, dinner and to bed — unless, of course, this first set of tests proved inconclusive.

The tests could be simple: look through the microscope, count cells killed by the antiserum in each of the plate's wells, score each field from one to eight by consulting a printed chart, and read down the chart for your genotypes.

And they might be simple: Mendelian law being what it was, each of a child's antigens was directly traceable to one or the other of its parents.

16

Best would be a classic Mendelian cross: four unique antigens from father, four from mother, while the other tested adults bore no antigens common to the child's, ruling out blood kinship as perfectly as examples from a genetics text.

If Helene's luck didn't run right, though, she would have to go on to track the chromosomal crossovers, antigen cross-reactivities, and gene-recombination frequencies. Worst case, she'd have to check out four sets of grandparents and who knew how many aunts and uncles, and end up swinging through four different family trees like a monkey in the jungle.

Helene sighed as she closed the incubator door. While these possibilities were troublesome, she knew they were also the basis for her place as chief technician in the immunology lab, so she could not entirely resent them.

Gregor Mendel hadn't had a clue about human immune response, which Helene sometimes suspected of generating new antigens just out of spite. Half the human tissue antigens — probably more — had not yet even been identified, and most techs didn't understand how to handle these unknowns when they showed up in a potential tissue match.

But Helene did. She couldn't explain just how she knew which immune system proteins, lurking on the white-cell surfaces, waited like shrapnel bombs to explode in a transplant patient's immune system. Still, she knew which serum reactions looked bad but were little more than saber-rattlings, which looked good yet were in truth murders waiting to be committed. Tissue matchings endorsed by herself had acceptance rates approaching 95 percent; the best other labs could do — on good days — was 75.

Questioned, Helene only laughed and said she could smell a white cell getting ready to pick a fight. Privately, though, she sometimes wondered if it happened to anyone else, the looking and looking, day in and day out, until she was no longer seeing cells but seeing into them. Human blood cells, stained, fixed in formalin: Helene saw them and felt, simply, a pricking in her thumbs.

Now, with the microtitre plates incubating and no others waiting to be processed, she set her watch timer for an hour, locked the lab, and headed downstairs to the hospital cafeteria. After lunching on a carton of blueberry yogurt and a bran muffin, she strolled to the credit union office, deposited a paycheck of $532.07, and took a flyer advertising low rates on loans for new or used cars.

Then she headed back past the pharmacy and the diagnostic-imaging departments, the clinical chemistry lab and the medical records room and the mail room, until she reached the basement of the building where her own lab was, twelve stories up.

Stepping from the elevator on the twelfth floor, she picked her way among coils of cable, stepladders, power tools, and dumpsters filled with torn-down sections of drywall, walking under yellow utility lamps strung haphazardly from dropcords. There was no sign of workmen, only a clutter of open toolboxes and an imperfectly swept-up mess of plaster dust with footprints tracked through it.

Helene wished they would hurry. On this floor, her lab alone had escaped the uproar of remodeling; with the others moved elsewhere until the job was done, working up here was a bit like working on the moon: isolated, and too silent.

Her watch beeped its one-hour reminder as she unlocked the lab and let herself in. Good, she thought, swinging the door shut behind her; a watched incubator never boiled.

Removing the warm T-cell plates and carrying them to the lab bench, she added five microliters of sticky tan rabbit-complement fluid to each well and set the plates aside. The rabbit serum would cause the killed cells to absorb stain so they could be seen and counted.

Next, she began the patient task of staining

and fixing the wells from plates she had prepared earlier, first adding five microliters of eosin, then an equal amount of formaldehyde fixative. Finally she relaid the glass slides over the rows of wells to flatten the seventy-two convex droplets in each typing plate.

Sixty minutes later she laid the first plate into the clips of the Leitz inverted microscope's heavy black viewing stage, adjusted the rheostat on the illuminator, and peered into the instrument's binocular eyepiece, adjusting the fine-focus knob as she did. Swiftly she began counting the killed cells in each viewing field, hardly glancing up as she noted the results on the first worksheet.

By a little after 3:00 P.M., all the T-cells had been counted. On the five worksheets, only columns labeled *Dr* remained unfilled. These columns were for the results of B-cell plates, the antigens occupying the fourth loci in each blood sample's immune-system fingerprint.

Staring at the letters and numbers in the grids already filled in, Helene felt the pricking of her thumbs spread into her wrists and begin shooting ominously toward her elbows. Bending to the eyepiece of the Leitz, she pronounced to herself the numbers of cells killed by the antisera in each well of the first B-cell plate, then made a note on the worksheet.

Filling in the *Dr* loci was like getting the final letters in a crossword puzzle or making visible a message written in invisible ink. Slowly, what had been hidden began to appear, each new symbol confirming a meaning that to Helene had already become obvious.

Really, she thought, how very unlikely and astonishing. And completely unarguable, for she had drawn all the samples herself and was sure there had been no mistake.

Bending for a last squint at the final field, she heard a small clicking sound behind her, almost like the sound of the thermostat she had been fiddling with earlier.

Only not quite like that.

Frowning, she raised her eyes from the microscope. Someone stood framed in the open doorway of the lab. Helene had an instant to know the face, but before she could put a name to it the clicking sound came again, then exploded in a bright white thunderclap.

Reaching out blindly, she found the worksheets and clutched at them, feeling them crumple wetly in her hand as she fell.

Good luck, honey, she thought as the explosion faded and the white light grew brighter.

Wondrously, unimaginably brighter.

TWO

The crack! of two rocks rapped sharply together underwater startled the small bright fish drifting in schools like neon clouds over the coral landscape. In a flashing instant they vanished into the waving green fields of turtlegrass and forests of sea cucumber.

Edwina Crusoe kicked once and ascended toward the wavery surface. Breaking through, she spat out the snorkel's mouthpiece and dragged her goggles back.

"What?" Above her loomed the *Bertram*'s white fiberglass hull. Tami had thrown the rope ladder over the side.

His lean, toast-brown face appeared at the rail. "Sorry," he said. In his hand was something that looked like a pocket radio with an aerial sticking up from one end. "Mainland."

"Blast." She kicked off her flippers, caught them before they could sink, and scrambled up the hemp rungs.

"Rough being indispensable," he agreed. Hauling the ladder up, he stowed it in the footlocker with the cushions and life preservers. "Catch your breath, I told them it'd be a few."

She dropped her gear on the canvas tarp and toweled her hair briefly with the coarse length of terry cloth he handed her. The warm Caribbean sun dried the droplets on her body, leaving small white salt circles that she brushed away.

"You should have told them I'd drowned."

Fastening the locker hasp, he grinned at her. "They'd never believe it." He picked up the can of polish and the cloth with which he had been lustering the aft bulkheads and gazed with sudden interest over the gunwale at the blank blue horizon.

"Go on, take it below before the sun fries you." He tossed the wireless phone at her. A moment later came the distant growl of diesel inboards, a white dot of spray appearing just outside the line of breakers at the lagoon's mouth.

The approaching craft found its way through the barrier reef and cut its engine as it drew alongside. It was an old Chris-Craft cruiser with dark-tinted windows, its foredecks and cabin trunk weathered to a pewterish teak-gray.

Edwina fished an icy bottle of TsingTao from the cockpit cooler and went below, pulling the sliding door shut behind her. Tami liked privacy for his business dealings, some of which came on abruptly and not all of which, she felt sure, involved being hand-somely paid for a couple of days' worth of easy skippering.

The aft cabin bristled with navigation gear: radar devices, sextants and compasses, weather gadgets, and a library of charts. Not for the first time, Edwina wondered what sort of contraband Tami made his living running.

It could hardly be drugs; in the many trips she had made here she had always chartered with Tami and had never seen him with so much as a single joint. But that didn't mean he was necessarily a stranger to other exotic transportables: rare shells, for instance, or the jewel-like chrysalises of tropical butterflies, whose prices were skyrocketing as their species edged steadily nearer to extinction.

In her own small cabin she sat cross-legged on the narrow bunk, drawing the curtain over the porthole, which at this time of day resembled a hot, staring eye. After several long swallows of the scouringly cold beer, she leaned the bottle on her bare leg and pressed the button on the wireless phone.

A brief electronic sputter was followed by the voice of the AT&T international operator, the satellite dish on the flying bridge overhead drawing the signal in as if it came from the island and not from two thousand miles away.

24

You can run but you can't hide, Edwina thought sourly, as a familiar voice came through the handset.

Returning to the above deck, she found the Chris-Craft gone and Tami locking the hatch on the aft hold.

"You look like you just stepped on a spiny urchin," he observed.

The beer had gone warm; she poured the rest over the lee rail. "Friend of mine's been hurt at home. Anyone flying out of Port Caribe that you know of? I have to go back."

Tami straightened. With his fierce white teeth and his hair blue-black in the hot sun, he looked like a modern-day pirate.

"Not unless you want to fly a powder-puff run."

It was local slang for a cocaine trip. The small planes took off from Panamanian carriers, skimmed in low, then island-hopped until they reached Port-au-Prince or one of the other distribution centers. From there the drug was muled a few kilos at a time into Miami — or, increasingly, along the less closely watched supply lines like the Marina Key-West Palm Beach route.

"They're fast," Tami said, "but sometimes they get shot down."

She shook her head. "I'll find a charter. If

I make it fast, I can get the night flight direct out of Kingston."

Tami considered. "Vinnie Cusano runs a milk and vegetable haul off Madrigal. We could call him."

"Uh-huh." She stared at the waves. "But first I'd have to get to Madrigal."

Tami's boat worked out of the island of San Jiralomo, a small mountainous atoll often uncharted and almost unknown to any but hard-bitten diving enthusiasts. Its only settlement boasted saloons, a dive shop, a ramshackle wooden hotel, and very little else. Getting on and off San Jiralomo took ingenuity, which was fine with Edwina except in emergencies.

"Vinnie can't fly in here, and if he did he couldn't fly out again," she said.

Frowning, Tami pretended to consider this, then vanished below. An instant later came the clatter of the anchor being raised, its chain reeling smoothly onto the power capstan, and the gurgly grumble of the *Bertram*'s 350-horse MerCruisers coming to life.

A sudden gust of diesel fumes reminded her why power boats were called stinkpots. Still, the *Bertram* was faster than any sailboat. Strapped into the companion benchseat with the banners snapping and the outriggers screaming overhead, she watched the water's surface drop away as the boat's stem nosed up.

"Not bad," she shouted. "What's she do, fifty?"

Tami shook his head, pushing forward on the throttle, which seemed — although of course that was ridiculous — to be up only about halfway.

Fifty knots was pretty good for a cruiser. Tami's mouth moved, but she couldn't hear what he said. He throttled up once more and the forty-foot *Bertram* seemed to gather itself in response, bunching its muscles for a lunge forward.

Then came a faint electronic whine, a whisper of resistance, and an amazing thing happened: the craft lifted onto the water and *skimmed* across it.

Hydroplane wings, Edwina realized: the smooth, tightly folded structures she had seen below the waterline but had been unable to identify. Now the *Bertram* was flying, just kissing the waves. Sixty-five knots, seventy.

Tami cut hard to starboard and spray flew up in a series of cold, brisk slaps. Green waters deepened to purple-black.

"What?" she shouted, cupping her ears.

"I said," he bellowed, "her top's around ninety. Never had her up that far, though. Want to try?"

What the hell. You could live an adventurous life and die having fun.

Or you could play it safe and get shot in the head in broad daylight, while supposedly secure inside Chelsea Memorial Hospital in New Haven, Connecticut.

She would be there, she calculated, in a little under twelve hours. "Let 'er rip!"

Behind and below, the MerCruisers howled like beasts out of their cages. Tami, his eyes and his grin stretched wide as they could go, throttled up a final time.

A *lot* faster.

In the gray predawn the Boeing 737 banked over the Hudson River, buzzed Manhattan from Times Square to its leg-turn over High Bridge Park, cleared the Triborough with, apparently, inches to spare, and dropped like a stone toward the East River.

Reminding herself that the pilot no doubt did this every morning, that he must be well trained and extremely experienced, Edwina studiously unclenched her stiff, white fingers from the armrests and began gathering her belongings.

Hours earlier she had taken off from an oiled-dirt runway, out of a soup-bowl crater surrounded by mountains and jungles of lush, sinister-looking greenery. The lurching ascent, accompanied by protests from the Cessna two-seater and curses from the hung-over pilot, had in no way resembled anything envisioned by Orville and Wilbur.

Nevertheless she preferred it to this landing at La Guardia, where the black waves rose up so fast she was sure she could read the labels on the bits of garbage bobbing in them in the long moments before the 737's wheels bumped reassuringly down.

In the terminal the wait for once was not interminable: she stood for just a few minutes while her papers were examined and her duffel rooted through by a sleepy customs clerk who blinked only at the line on her visa listing her occupation as "registered nurse."

Dressed in dark Levi's and boots, a black leather bomber jacket over a white silk shirt and a rope of turquoise and beaten-silver lumps at her throat, Edwina knew she must not look like a nurse to him. She apparently also didn't resemble someone who hid cocaine or marijuana among her underthings, for after a cursory check and a final puzzled glance he waved her on through.

Feeling the mild euphoria of someone who has, in rapid succession, descended safely from 37,000 feet and been declared street-legal by a U.S. government official, she hoisted her duffel and proceeded to the long-term parking lot. There she found the Fiat Spider just as she had left it: black canvas top unslit, apricot paint unmarred, head and tail lights all present and intact.

This seemed a miracle until she spotted the seven buff tags stuck under the driver's side windshield wiper. It appeared that she had parked the Spider in a spot that was For Official Use Only — an offense carrying a fifty-dollar-a-day fine.

Ticketing her for this offense was clearly unreasonable. Of course she was using the space officially. She was parked in it, wasn't she? Stacking the summonses neatly one atop the other, she tore the entire pile into twenty-eight eminently satisfying pieces and dropped them into a trash bin marked Fine For Littering: $25.

Gratified at having saved $375 instead of only $350 — by not spitting in the subway, she calculated, she could raise the total to $400 — she fired up the Fiat and roared down the concrete ramp, heading for the lane marked 678 — Whitestone Bridge — New England.

By the time she got onto the bridge, however, her pleasure was extinguished by the memory of why she was returning to New Haven. Also, she lacked exact change for the toll. Sighing, she edged the Fiat into the line backed up from the booth marked Attendant On Duty, hoping as she did so that this wasn't an omen for the day.

But it was, as she discovered a few moments later when the little car began listing gently but irrevocably to the left, a signal generally employed by the Fiat to let her know that one of its Michelins was flattening. She could change the tire here in the middle of the Whitestone or limp on through the toll to the shoulder, a process that would inevitably warp the rim.

Slamming out of the car, she yanked the jack and lug wrench from behind the driver's seat and stomped around to the trunk. As she removed the spare, the honking began: first brief nudging toots, then long earsplitting blares.

Which was how she knew, aside from a clear mental picture of a seventeen-year-old girl with a bullet in her brain —

Which was how she knew, the marrow-shriveling blast of an eighteen-wheeler's air horn now confirming this utterly and completely —

Which was how Edwina Crusoe knew that she was no longer in paradise.

31

THREE

By seven-thirty the sky had lightened to pale gray and a few snowflakes were swirling dispiritedly out of it. With New Haven Harbor glinting on her right and the railyards of Union Station spreading soot-smudged on her left, Edwina urged the Fiat into the fast lane of I-95, as owing to the vision of some highway designer from hell, this was also the downtown exit ramp.

Minutes later, having parked in a municipal garage, she was striding down a glassed-in walkway toward Chelsea Memorial Medical Center. On either side of the walkway the buildings of the medical complex crowded in a familiar jumble, the fluted pillars and marble facade of Winchester Medical Library giving way to the red brick Dickensian sprawl of Brady Psychiatric Institute, the glassy futuristic towers of the Howard Hughes Research Pavilion springing absurdly from a cluster of contractors' Quonsets still huddled on the site. Just ahead lay the hospital itself, a dozen stories of creamy glazed brick looming over a half-circle drive clogged with taxis and medi-vans.

Making her way against an exiting stream of haggard night-shift workers, Edwina flashed her employee ID at the lobby guard and went in past the gift shop, coffee shop, and information desk to a house phone on the wall by the visitors' elevators. There, punching in the extension of the nursing desk in the surgical intensive care unit, she learned that yesterday's gunshot-wound victim had been sent to the operating room only moments ago.

The patient was so unstable that the neurosurgeons hadn't wanted to take the case at all, the charge nurse elaborated when she recognized Edwina's voice, but when the patient's cardiac complexes started widening out and they decided not going might be worse than going, they bumped an elective aneurysm clipping off the top of the OR schedule and stuck her on as an emergency case instead, making no promises and saying nothing about when — or if — they might return with her.

In her mind's eye Edwina saw clearly the green-tiled surgical suite, stately rituals of prep all fast-forwarded to quickstep: instrument trays placed and opened, gauze packets torn, solutions drawn and mixed, and labeled syringes laid out in order of use.

Meanwhile the patient's head would be shaved, cleansed, and draped, the incision performed in a single curving stroke, the scalp peeled back and clamped to expose the skull. After a while you got used to the noise the bone-saw made, if you were an OR nurse long enough.

Next the surface of the brain itself would appear, the bleeding controlled with sponges, suction, and cautery. Over the hours of dissection and excavation still to come, the bullet would be found, isolated, and plucked out with forceps; dropping into the specimen basin, it would make a faint clinking sound.

Unless the patient expired before then, in which case the bullet would be removed at postmortem examination as required by state law governing deaths resulting from homicide.

Edwina punched another extension. The nursing administration secretary answered on the first ring.

"Yes, Miss Crusoe, she's here. She asked me to let you know she'd like to see you as soon as you got in, but someone's with her at the moment. Will half an hour from now be all right?"

Which only confirmed what Edwina already knew: Julia Friedlander wanted something. She wanted it badly, she wanted it now, and she wanted it from Edwina; otherwise no call would have reached the *Bertram* in the first place.

Agreeing to appear as requested, Edwina hung up and took the elevator upstairs. No doubt there were worse jobs than second in command and chief troubleshooter to a tough old warhorse like Julia Friedlander, but just at the moment she couldn't think of what they were.

At the start of a day shift the hallways of the clinical wards resembled some cutthroat game of bumper car: wheelchairs and stretchers, medication carts and X-ray machines, dietary trucks and OR gurneys all jostling for a clear shot to or from the service elevators while the nurses threaded their harried way between like so many extra-point targets.

The only vehicle absent from the fray was the news vendor's wagon. Edwina scanned the nursing desk but didn't see what she wanted, so with motives she recognized as only faintly malicious she continued into the clean utility room.

There she found three nurses' aides already hard at work refurbishing their nail polish and teaching one another new dance steps and a pair of orderlies huddled intently over the sports pages. Music blared from a portable radio in an incomprehensible blur.

Snapping off the radio, Edwina snatched the newspaper up with one hand and brushed a pile of Lee Press-On Nails into the lap of the nearest aide with the other. "Scat," she said, thinking hard and hopefully of Lee Nail-On Nails.

Blinking in resentment, they sloped off. Edwina recapped a bottle of acetone left open on the utility counter, dropped a cotton ball stained Berry Berry Red into the trash, and poured herself a Styrofoam cupful of the noxious brown liquid lurking in the coffee urn. Then she sat, opening the confiscated newspaper to the front page.

TECH DIES, VOLUNTEER CRITICAL IN HOSPITAL SHOOTING
Hospital Defends Security Procedures, Says Attack "Unpreventable"

34-year-old lab technician Helene Motavalli was fatally shot and a hospital volunteer critically wounded early Tuesday afternoon in a twelfth-floor laboratory at Chelsea Memorial Hospital. Grace Savarin, 17, remained in "very critical" condition in the hospital's surgical intensive care unit Tuesday night, while surgery to remove a .22-caliber bullet from her brain was postponed until her condition stabilized. The unknown attacker

(Continued on page 2, column 2)

36

Glancing at her watch, Edwina scanned the rest of the story. It was always best before meeting with Julia Friedlander to have one's ducks in a row — as many, at any rate, as one could gather on such short notice.

Meanwhile the newspaper had gotten its facts down quite well, she thought: an isolated lab, the sudden calling to account of hospital security, shock over the critical injury to a young volunteer who was described on the continuing page as the "pride of William Penn High and a cheerful, familiar face in the neighborhood where she lived with her family."

No motive for the attack was known, nor had the intruder's method of entering and leaving the hospital yet been detected. But it was a detail left unmentioned that interested Edwina most.

Thoughtful, she refolded the newspaper. The medical center comprised a great many buildings, almost all possessing at least twelve floors and many of them housing laboratories.

Replacing the paper on the utility-room table — after all, there was no sense being a dog in the manger about it — she couldn't help wondering which laboratory it was, precisely, that someone had thought should remain unnamed at least for the present.

And — why?

★ ★ ★

Chelsea Memorial's offices of nursing administration were located in the Boardman Building, the last surviving relic of the original Chelsea Hospital. Erected in 1842, its forty-bed wards boasted marble-tiled floors, oak wainscoting, high vaulted ceilings that curved down into tall arched windows, and enormous coal-burning fireplaces.

Stoking and banking the fires in those fireplaces, filling the oil lamps and polishing their glass chimneys, and maintaining a proper supply of trimmed wicks had all been nursing duties in those days, along with sponging foreheads, rolling bandages, and spooning-out such powders, tinctures, and syrups as were available — chiefly crude herb preparations and laudanum.

Now the enormous fireplaces had been plastered over, the long wards divided by wallboard into offices and meeting rooms. The small black-and-white octagonal tiles had been covered too, with green linoleum waxed so bright that Edwina could see the sole of her shoe in it with every step.

But the wainscoting had been spared, along with the tall wavery-glass windows that gathered in the light as they arched to the vaulted ceilings, so that when one walked down a corridor of the Boardman Building it seemed a

38

hint of carbolic still floated in the air, accompanied perhaps by the ghostly rustle of starched uniform aprons, hushed voices of women addressing one another as sister.

Edwina thought the new buildings with their private rooms, fluorescent lighting, and banks of cardiac-monitor screens were much more efficient and convenient than this antique area. In the old days, if you opened one of these windows — which you did only in daylight, of course; evening vapors were known to be injurious — you propped it open with a stick.

She also thought that the average sick person had about as much chance of getting well all alone in a private room — loomed over by frightening bits of medical technology, blown upon by chill or super-heated air from a ventilator duct, and snapped at by a disembodied voice over an intercom speaker — as the average bug had of getting well in a jar full of chloroform-cotton, evening vapors or no evening vapors.

All of which made what Julia Friedlander was saying now very interesting indeed.

". . . retire," Julia said.

Seated behind her gray metal desk, her plump wrinkled face, blue-rinsed curls, and gold wire-rimmed spectacles made her resemble someone's harmless old cookie-baking

39

grandmother, an impression she corrected each time she reamed out some fresh-mouthed young physician or hapless medical student. She had been director of nursing at Chelsea for as long as almost anyone could remember.

Soon, though, someone else would take over.

"Indeed," Julia said, replying shrewdly to this thought of Edwina's, for while her eyes might be old they missed little. "The board of directors has asked me to propose my successor — a great honor, and one I have accepted." She looked at Edwina. "I intend proposing you."

"Thank you," Edwina said, hearing alarm bells in her head.

How remarkably interesting. Julia hadn't timed a murder to coincide with her retirement; therefore, she was timing her retirement to coincide with murder.

Or at least timing her announcement of it.

Steepling her fingers, pursing her lips judiciously, Julia shot a measuring glance at the pair of plainclothes police officers standing in attendance before her.

The tall one was McIntyre. The short one was Talbot. Both of them looked official, impatient, and slightly confused as to why they were hearing any of this at all.

40

"Meanwhile hospital security will of course assist these detectives," Julia said, "in their investigation of yesterday's outrage. But if they need further help they're to come to you."

Edwina nodded at the officers and saw them assessing how much help or hindrance she might be. So this is what Julia wants, she thought, or part of it: the direct approach.

Which still did not explain why she wanted it, but Edwina suspected that too would soon be made clear.

"Oh, and one other thing," Julia said mildly, almost as an afterthought.

The message at least was crystal clear: you handle this for me now, and I'll hand you my job, later. Otherwise . . .

But otherwise did not bear thinking of. Edwina wanted to be the director of nursing, had wanted it in fact for a very long time. She wanted the status and title, the perks and the power, but most of all she wanted the chance to make changes.

Four-bed wards on some of the general-care floors; a little commiseration and watching out for one another had never hurt any sick people she'd ever heard of. Call lights answered by human beings, not intercoms. Windows that opened, damn it.

The chance to make a difference: Julia was

offering it with a catch. It started now, immediately.

The officer named McIntyre cleared his throat. He was bony, hawk-faced, and narrow-lipped, with a dark receding hairline and sharp dark eyes.

"We understand you're acquainted with one of the victims," he said. "The surviving victim, Grace Savarin."

Edwina nodded. "Grace started as a high-school volunteer. They come in a couple of evenings, sometimes Saturdays, to help in the gift shop or play with the pediatric patients. That sort of thing."

Which did not even begin to explain Grace, who had done so much more almost as soon as she arrived. Her endless energy, her habit of reading up on things she didn't understand, puzzling over them until she did —

Grace, in fact, had made everything seem possible again, simply by seeing it so. "She's an unusual girl," Edwina said inadequately, banishing an unwanted vision of where Grace was right now.

"Any idea what she might have been doing in the tissue-typing lab? Isn't that pretty far off the beaten track?"

"Yes, I suppose so," Edwina began, "but Grace liked to ask questions, find out how all kinds of things — "

42

She stopped. So that was what this was about. "The Dietz-Claymore case," she said to Julia, who nodded unhappily.

"The results of the blood tests were to be delivered to the court today," Julia said. "So far the newspapers haven't picked up on the connection, but that won't last."

"And the tests themselves? The material?"

"Gone."

The second detective — Talbot, his name was — frowned down at his notebook. "Fifteen collection tubes, a dozen tissue-typing plates, and five histo-compatibility worksheets," he recited.

"I see," Edwina said slowly. The air in the room seemed suddenly still and clear. "Yes, I do think I see how this might be extremely difficult for everyone." And why Julia had thought her particular skills might be useful.

At the same time, her nomination as Chelsea's next director of nursing would not be a popular one. Four solid strikes against her:

Too young; although at thirty-five she no longer thought of herself as particularly junior.

Too pretty; knowing she did not resemble a gargoyle, she knew others judged her appearance rather better, and of course suspected her for it.

Too rich; money made people independent, and of course the board did not like that one bit.

And too stubborn. Most of all too stubborn. Nurses were supposed to be sweet, compliant, and amenable to orders, while Edwina knew herself to be tart, resistant, and habitually argumentative.

All of which might still be overcome if only she could show some ability the board thought desirable: an ability to end this nastiness very quickly and with a minimum of fuss and bother, for instance.

She turned to the tall policeman. "You'll need to know about tissue-typing first of all, I think. The possibilities of it, I mean, what it can and can't really do. Why don't I begin there, and perhaps I can have something for you later today."

His eyes weren't dark at all, she saw now, but pale gray; only the shadow of his brow had made them appear dark. As he nodded minutely and with comprehension, she thought he might even turn out to be astute.

That would be good, she thought, although in the long run it hardly mattered.

"What," she asked Julia, "is the other thing?"

"The Dietzes and the Claymores," said Julia

Friedlander when the officers had gone, "are going to sue this hospital the minute they understand what's happened. They may even band together to do so, despite their differences. Among other things, they'll say our security was inadequate, which it may or may not have been, and that they've suffered serious pain and emotional distress."

She sighed. "Which I suppose they will by the time this is over, I don't know. People hear the word 'hospital,' they smell money. But the point is, defending oneself against even a frivolous action can be expensive, troublesome, and extremely damaging to one's reputation, as this morning's newspaper has only begun to show."

Edwina frowned. "I don't see what I can do about it. Besides, Chelsea's been sued before and survived."

"Indeed," Julia replied. "But I'm afraid at present the attendant publicity would be most inconvenient. You see, the cardiothoracic people want to lure a chest surgeon named Walter Wilkins here to head up a new heart-lung transplant program. If we should become embroiled in some unpleasant newsworthiness — well, Wilkins has had an experience along those lines once before, you may recall."

She did recall. "At Loma Linda. Got sued for a couple of million by some patient's estate

— they said he botched the surgery because he was drunk or something."

"Or something," Julia agreed. "He was found blameless, but first he was dragged through the courts and the tabloids along with a number of his girlfriends, and — so it was said — boyfriends."

"An active fellow," Edwina observed.

"Quite so. But the fellow we need to get a new transplant program, and he won't come if there's a bad aroma of any sort."

"You still haven't said what you think I can do about it."

Julia pursed her lips. "This McIntyre man seems capable enough," she allowed. "But the death of a medical technician in a hospital, in the midst of some rather sophisticated medical testing — not to mention a theft of tissue material — well. It does rather suggest a medical motive, doesn't it?" She looked at Edwina. "Meanwhile, medicine is hardly a subject in which most policemen are well versed."

"So," Edwina said slowly, "you want an end run. I get the story, or however much of it I can, and feed it to McIntyre to get him on track fast."

"Precisely," said Julia. "Wilkins visits next week. If he doesn't like what he finds, he won't be back. He isn't doing very well at Loma Linda, I hear. He's not getting funds, equipment, cases — he's under a sort of cloud there, despite having been cleared legally. At Chelsea he can start over and help us, too — unless we find ourselves under a similar cloud."

"I understand," Edwina said, following the older woman to the office door. "How frequently would you like me to report to you on this?"

Julia paused, her hand on the knob. "Report to me," she replied with a look of bland innocence, "on what?"

"I d-demuh-mand to know wh-what's going on. W-we were all h-here yesterday — wh-why were we c-called b-back?" Oliver Dietz's pale, freckled face twisted painfully with his effort to force the words out. "H-have the t-test results c-c-come in?"

The floor of the pediatric playroom was littered with bright blue Smurfs, metal Go-Bots, and pastel My Little Ponies. A small wheelchair and an IV pole on rollers stood in one corner, a grip of gauze and tape wrapped around the pole's upright where a four-year-old might grasp it.

It was after 10:00 A.M. Edwina would have liked to find another place for this meeting, but the cafeteria was too public and the conference rooms all were occupied: a Lamaze class, two groups of SmokeEnders, a Reach for Recovery, and a presurgery transsexual mutual-support session.

In fact she would have liked to skip the meeting altogether, but she wanted a look at the warring families. Now that she had one, her first impression was that the Dietzes and Claymores were about as likely to band together on anything as the Hatfields and the McCoys.

Still, they could always sue separately. Besides, someone had to break the news to them.

"M-my daughter — " Dietz began again. He wore a blue off-the-rack suit, a yellowed polyester shirt slightly fraying at the too-short cuffs, and a red clip-on bow tie.

"Oh, no you don't," Jane Claymore broke in, her harsh voice murdering Dietz's effort at speech. She looked like a picture snipped from a slick, expensive catalog: trim slacks, white oxford-cloth shirt, a navy cardigan casually draped across her shoulders. Diamond studs twinkled in her earlobes.

"I've heard just about enough out of you — you bumpkins." Her smooth dark hair swung angrily as she snatched up a green Bic lighter, firing another in her endless chain of cigarettes and spewing a stream of smoke. "He looks," she observed venomously to no one in particular, "like Howdy Doody."

Beside Jane Claymore's brittle elegance, Margaret Dietz's jeans and sweater seemed shabbier and more shapeless than they were. Her hair, wispy and mouse-colored, had been hacked at with scissors; her forehead was wide and shiny above green, slightly protuberant eyes. On her feet were an old pair of rubber boots; her large, chapped hands gripped her coffee cup, which now looked in imminent danger of being hurled at Jane Claymore's face.

"She's not your child," Jane Claymore persisted. "Haven't you done enough damage in that hillbilly shack of yours? Raising her with chickens and pigs — you don't even send her to school."

This, from what Edwina had learned of the Claymores and the Dietzes, wasn't quite true. Oliver Dietz instructed the little girl at home, a task for which his advanced degrees in education equipped him more than adequately. Margaret Dietz did much of the work on their farm, where they raised sheep whose wool she spun and sold by mail order to weaving and crafts enthusiasts. But the part about chickens and pigs *was* partly accurate, for while the chickens lived in chicken coops, the pigs — pet pigs, trained miniature ones, two of them — had the run of the house.

"No cultural opportunities, no social advantages . . . ," Jane Claymore nattered endlessly between sharp puffs on her cigarette.

"That's enough," her husband broke in, "we've heard all that before." William Claymore's tone was that of a grown-up bringing a roomful of kindergarteners to reluctant order. "Miss Crusoe is here to tell us what's going on," he said. "Suppose we just let her try, shall we?"

As he spoke, his bullet-shaped head of close-clipped silver hair thrust forward challengingly. His good charcoal suit had not come out of a catalog, nor had the white silk shirt or the tricolor school tie he wore with such natural authority.

Edwina, who had an eye for these things, thought the suit had been tailored for him in Hong Kong, along with shirts bought two or more dozen at a time. The tie was just another signal of the power Claymore radiated, quietly but emphatically; I can do, his large calm presence seemed to say, whatever I need to do.

"Fine," she said. "If that's what you all want," she added. With a lift of his salt-and-pepper eyebrows, Claymore accepted this, and his wife too fell silent, at least for the present.

Swiftly, Edwina outlined the events of the previous day. Three pairs of eyes widened, three jaws dropped as she explained what had been taken from the tissue lab. Only Claymore listened motionlessly, his expression one of thoughtful interest and utter comprehension.

"This is *outrageous* — "

"The hospital," Edwina said, steamrollering smoothly over Jane Claymore's protests, "is aware that these developments are very stressful for you. There are ways we can help, and I'll try to identify them and make them available to you as soon as possible."

" — *criminal* — "

Claymore's eyes remained unfooled.

"But first," Edwina went on imperturbably, for she made it a rule never to swat the living daylights out of a person no matter how badly that person needed it, "I want to be sure I understand your situation, so I'll need to ask a few brief — "

"Oh," Jane Claymore wailed, "we've *been* through this and *been* through — "

"Shut up, Jane," her husband advised genially.

The effect was instantaneous: Jane Claymore's mouth snapped shut, her slim shoulders cringing as if beneath an expected blow. Edwina wondered if pretty Jane's strong, take-charge husband ever slapped her around a little. Not hard, just hard enough to stop that dentist-drill whine.

Oliver Dietz watched, too, clearly out of his depth and wanting only to escape from these people. He struggled with the attempt to begin a sentence, but his wife beat him to it.

"You don't know, do you?" Margaret Dietz's pale-lashed green eyes were surprisingly sharp and observant. "About us, I mean," she went on. "Only what you read in the papers, I'll bet. Now this happens, you're here to check us out. See if anyone's yelling about a lawsuit. Yet," she added.

This appraisal, so succinct and so accurate, left Edwina with nothing to do but nod. Even Claymore looked impressed.

"Well, I'll tell," Margaret Dietz said. "I don't mind, the whole thing's simple. It won't take long."

"I could tell you who's simple," Jane Claymore muttered with a testing glance at her husband, who ignored her.

Margaret Dietz went on as if she hadn't heard. "Four years back the Claymores' little girl got sick. Her name was Jill and she was five, same as our Hallie."

And there, thought Edwina, lies the rub.

"Tests showed the trouble was in her liver," Margaret Dietz said, "and she needed a new one, a transplant. So naturally they did all those other tests, to show whose parts will match up with whose, and whose won't."

Her voice was a natural storyteller's voice,

52

rich and musical, rising and falling with events. "Tests came back," she shook her head, "nobody could believe it. But they were true."

She looked around the table. "This little Jill, she wasn't the Claymores' blood kin." She shook her head. "No one thought that before, and no one would've. Only the tests showed it for sure, you see.

"It meant she wasn't their real child. But of course they didn't care about that — not then. They just wanted to get her well."

Jane Claymore lit another cigarette.

"Only," Margaret Dietz went on, "she didn't get well. She got worse, and they never did find a new liver that would work for her. And then this little girl — who no one ever learned who she really was or where she really came from — this child died, finally."

The room was very still. Jane Claymore stared tight-lipped at her burning cigarette, while her husband's face was impassive. Oliver Dietz looked sad.

"Anyway, they'd already figured out they'd got the wrong baby at the hospital. Only not by accident. On purpose, a sick one for a healthy one. For money."

"We didn't 'figure' it, it's been proven." Jane Claymore's voice was torn with remembered grief. "But," she added, "the birth certificates and records were faked or destroyed."

And that, Edwina remembered, was the part that had been in all the newspapers. Scandal at a private obstetrical clinic, babies of unwed mothers given to couples whose own died at birth. At the start, two or three such transactions had seemed to solve a lot of problems with a minimum of difficulty.

But then someone had figured out there was profit in it; lots of people, as it happened, wanted newborn white infants and were willing to pay, confidentially, the medical expenses of some unfortunate unwed girl to get one.

Which was how the real trouble began. Charity cases, poor farmers, or factory-working parents were told that their infants had died. With Mom drugged to grogginess and Dad sequestered in the waiting room during the contrived emergency, that part was easy enough.

Parents asking to see a dead child were told that, because of the lifesaving measures taken on its behalf, the newborn's looks were now most unfortunate. Privately, each parent was also told that the sight would be damaging to the other.

None insisted; patients at the Albemarle Clinic were for the most part unschooled and credulous — except of course for the Clay-mores, who were simply in the wrong place at the wrong time.

Driving home from a weekend excursion when Jane Claymore's labor pains began, they had found the clinic, entered in fear at the three-weeks' early arrival of their first child, and departed five days later with Jill.

After Jill's death, followed by the explosion of the scandal and the suicide of the clinic's medical director, they had spent two years hunting children who might be their real daughter: white, female, and born at the clinic within a few days of Jane's confinement.

Finally they had found one: Hallie Dietz.

"Th-there were f-four other babies," Oliver Dietz said, "but they only l-located three. And one was bluh-black."

"There were not four," Jane Claymore said, exasperated. "I was there, I ought to know if there were — "

"You," Margaret Dietz said, "were out cold. Yelled so loud for painkillers, the nurses went an' gave 'em to you, knocked you flat out."

"That's another lie — "

"Besides us," said Margaret, "there was that great big fat lady who cussed out her poor little husband every time she got a pain. And the one with eight youngsters to home, she's the one should have been cussing, but she never did. And then the black lady, Hepzibah Scott. Pretty name. 'Lord, I'm hot,' she kept saying. 'Lord, it's hot in here.' All night long."

She smiled reminiscently. "Finally, that real young girl was brought in. All alone, dead scared and crying. And Hepzibah Scott said, 'Girl, you stop crying. Sit up, now, and act like a righteous woman.' And the girl did. She was all right after that."

"You," said Jane Claymore, stabbing accusingly with her cigarette, "are making up every bit of that. There was no girl, and how would you know if there was one? You went to the operating room, even you admit that much."

Margaret Dietz nodded. "Which is where our Hallie was born. By cesarean section, at 5:54 A.M. on July 12th, and I've got the scar to prove it."

"But," Edwina put in, "these tests were ordered to settle the Claymores' claim. To prove Hallie's biological parentage, one way or another. Isn't that right?"

"Th-that's right," Oliver Dietz managed. "W-we decided we might as well j-just get it over with."

His chin came up; he put his hand on his wife's arm. "They m-made a mistake, th-that's all. D-don't worry, Maggie, we aren't g-going to lose Hallie."

"Our lawyers assure us the court will award custody to us," Jane Claymore said acidly. "She's ours, after all."

"Jane," her husband said, "that's not quite accurate, you know. Some sort of joint custody might be instituted."

"Tissue tests," Margaret Dietz said placidly, as if no one else had spoken. "Because, as it turns out, we all are just the same blood type, so that's no help."

Edwina blinked. "You don't know what will happen? The judge hasn't told you what the outcome will be, whichever way the test results go?"

Claymore shook his head. "That's been the holdup, or one of them." He eyed the Dietzes sternly. "I've put a lot of time and money into this, you realize, this isn't frivolous on my part."

Jane Claymore sniffed. "Obviously they must have something to hide. Otherwise why not have the tests done at once, instead of making us force them into it?" She leaned across the table. "And it won't be over with if there's any idea of joint custody, I guarantee you that."

"And if the tests don't prove what you think they will?" Edwina ventured. Which of course they might not; without some claim on both sides, none of it could have come this far.

After all, Jane Claymore was right about one thing: if the Dietzes were as sure of themselves as they said, why not just have the proof gathered and be done with it? Instead they had fought, delaying the procedure almost two years.

On the other hand, there was Jane herself: implacable as some predatory bird, ready to swoop down and snatch a child from the only home and parents she had ever known.

And then there was William Claymore, who without his wife's insistence would have had little if any interest in Hallie Dietz; of that Edwina was already quite certain.

Here was no longer the eager young husband of ten years ago but a prosperous businessman, settled and satisfied. A generous, carefully administered trust fund, perhaps even some minimal visiting arrangement: that would be Claymore's style of fatherhood now, Edwina felt sure, if he even exerted himself to so much involvement.

No, Jane Claymore was the nettle in this thicket, along with something that remained as yet unrevealed.

Something plain but unseen, Edwina thought, like a child's picture puzzle: how many faces can you find hidden in these clouds?

"I've lost one baby," Jane Claymore asserted. "I won't lose another." She opened her mouth as if to say more.

"I think," her husband put in swiftly, "there's someone else who wants to talk to us. Am I right, Miss Crusoe?"

His look said he knew the answer, had known it, in fact, all along. Shooting his cuffs impatiently, he glanced at his Rolex like a man who has already spent too much time humoring his underlings.

"The police," he said, glancing around the table as if this must be obvious. "Seeing," he added, "as we are now all suspects in a murder."

FOUR

"Imagine," Harry Lemon said, "that your immune system is run by the nastiest, meanest, most murderous cells in your entire body. Which it is. And they are."

Escaping from the conference room to the wards of Seven West, Edwina had found Harry at the nursing desk with dozens of charts spread out before him and thought herself fortunate. Being taught by Harry required the casting off of a great many preconceived notions, but it was also a fast way to learn almost everything about almost anything.

As he spoke, his fountain pen moved across the chart pages: scribbling progress notes, renewing medication orders, filling out consult requests, and signing X-ray requisitions.

"Immune-system cells," he said, scrawling something that a thousand signatures ago might just possibly have resembled his name, "hate everything that is not exactly like themselves."

Harry was fortyish, plump and balding, with a pink rosebud mouth and a grave, professional manner punctuated by legendary fits of temper. As an immunology specialist he treated patients with AIDS, chronic cancers, or — now that AIDS patients were living long enough to develop chronic cancers — both.

"Any time their turf is invaded by a foreign cell," Harry continued, "savage tribes of immune cells spread out through the bloodstream to hunt the invader down and kill it."

"Right," she said. "White blood cells, I get that part."

"But," Harry asked, brushing away her interruption, "how do the killer cells know? How can they tell when they run into a cell — or even part of one — that it isn't one of *them?*"

Smiling, he answered his own question. "They're all wearing protein ID badges, that's how, and so are all the other cells in your body — each one wears eight little ID badges called antigens, and the badges say, in essence, Don't kill me — I belong here.

"So," he went on, "if the white cells see badges that don't belong — foreign cells, bearing antigens that aren't your own — well, then. Mayhem, better known as the immune response, ensues."

Edwina nodded. "All right, but now we get to where I need a brushup. There are seventy-five or so different human tissue antigens, correct? But each person carries only eight of them?"

"Correct," Harry said. "That's why your antigens might all be different from mine, and the fellow down the hall might have eight different ones still."

He waved an expressive hand. "Or we all three might by chance have some in common — perhaps even quite a few in common, which is what organ transplants between unrelated people depend on. And that's what tissue typing does: finds out who shares at least some antigens — called, by the way, human leukocyte antigens."

He finished another note on another chart. "And the way you get your antigens is straightforward, too — you inherit them. Four from your father and four from your mother."

She nodded. "So if I've got a certain antigen, either my mother or my father has it, too. Had to have, to pass it along to me. Maybe both of them have it. But if neither one does . . ."

"Then one of them is not in fact your father or mother." He opened another chart. "Now, if that's sufficient — "

But it wasn't. Something about the whole business remained troublesome, only she couldn't quite put her finger on what.

Meanwhile a ferocious scowl began spreading on Harry's face. "You," he said, glowering past her.

Turning, she found a mailman standing at the nursing desk. At least, he was wearing a mailman's uniform with a red-and-gold eagle piped on the blue serge sleeve, and he was gripping the handle of a mailman's three-wheeled letter cart.

But on his face was a most unmailmanlike look of fear and heels-dug-in mulishness. "I told you before, Dr. Lemon," he said, "I'm not taking it. You can wrap it in plastic or dip it in chemicals or I don't care what you do, but I'm not and that's that."

A flush climbed Harry's neck. "You," he exploded, "are an idiot!"

The mailman stood his ground. "Uh-huh. That's what you say. All I know is I'll probably get fired. On account," he added in an injured tone, "of that guy."

Edwina looked down the corridor where the mailman pointed but found no guys in evidence, only the TV-lady with her little black charge book, a volunteer pushing a cart heaped with magazines, and a lab runner lugging a basket of fluid-filled jars.

"What about your appointed rounds?" Harry demanded. "What about through sleet and snow and dark of night?"

"Nobody ever said anything about through germs," retorted the mailman. "AIDS germs," he amplified, turning to Edwina, "crawlin' all over the envelopes, licked on the stamps, there. No sirree, I don't want any contact with them at *all*."

"Our friend," Harry explained in disgust, "has discovered an AIDS patient on this ward. One who wishes to send mail, as I believe is still his right as a citizen."

"Stacks of it," the mailman put in indignantly. "Heaps of it, every day. I got rights too, you know. I guess," he added unhappily, "I got the right to go try and find a new job now."

"Wait a minute," Edwina said, still distracted by thoughts of killer immune cells, inherited badges, and something that did not — could not — quite make good sense.

Harry and the mailman looked at her. "What?" they asked together, Harry grimly and the mailman with a tinge of hope.

Drat. Whatever didn't make sense was right on the tip of her tongue; she would have to concentrate on something else to unblock it.

Thinking this, she turned back to the two of them. "Harry," she said, "you are such an excellent teacher. In addition to your remarkable clinical skills, of course."

At this, Harry gave a faint wriggle of pleasure.

"And you," she said to the mailman, "only

want to protect yourself, which is something I quite understand, too."

"Right," the mailman said, "*I* only want to — "

"So," she continued, "I think Harry should give us a brief demonstration. After which, if he is successful, you'll take the mail. But only of your own free will," she added, "and only if you really think it's safe.

"But," she raised an admonishing finger at Harry, "if you don't convince him, he doesn't have to take it, and you won't complain about him. We'll find some other way of handling this mail, and we won't say another word about it. Agreed?"

Harry's lips curved upward as the gist of the plan struck him. Meanwhile the more the mailman understood the less he liked it, but a little thing like someone else's fear had never stopped Harry before — it was, in fact, the standard emotional backdrop for most of his work — and clearly he was not about to let it stop him now.

Heaving himself from his chair, tugging at the rumpled green scrub suit he wore — Harry maintained that since he never knew when he would manage to get any sleep, his clothes might just as well always resemble pajamas — he rubbed his fingers together in pleased anticipation.

"Come along, children," he intoned. "It's show time."

"This," the mailman complained, "is against my better judgment."

"Don't be silly, you don't have any judgment."

Harry tugged on the strings of the mailman's isolation gown, tying them.

The rest of the costume, devised by Harry to provide the maximum in mailman confidence, consisted of a surgical cap and mask, pull-on paper shoe covers, goggles, and latex gloves — at the mailman's insistence, three layers of latex gloves.

"There," Harry said. "No virus could even find you, much less infect you."

Behind the goggles the mailman's eyes were anxious. "Sure, that's what you say. If I had my pension vested, no way I'd —"

"Oh, shut up and come along," Harry snapped, "before I decide again to stop suffering fools gladly." Rapping once on the door of his patient's room, he urged the mailman in.

Full of doubt, Edwina followed. All at once this didn't seem like such a good idea: invading a sick person's privacy to make a public-health lesson out of him.

Harry, however, harbored no such doubts. "Good afternoon, Mr. Williams," he boomed, or perhaps it was only that the room was so tiny and so full.

Cards and posters, notes and snapshots papered one whole wall, while the space between bed and windowsill bristled with IV poles, tube-feeding apparatus, an aluminum walker, and a commode. The air in the room smelled of peppermint, heavy over something else.

Blinking, the man in the bed gazed up at them.

"This," Harry told him, "is Miss Crusoe, a nurse at our fine institution, and this fellow here is your mailman."

"Porter," supplied the mailman uncomfortably. "Tim Porter."

"Ah, yes. Mr. Porter. He's not in an institution yet," Harry confided, "but we're working on it."

"Harry," said Edwina, "perhaps Mr. Williams doesn't care to be a — "

"Guinea pig," said Williams. His eyes were bright and blue, like huge gems in his skeletally thin face. "Don't worry. Harry's promised to keep me alive as long as I let him teach on me, and so far he's made good on his end of the deal. Call me Brady, by the way."

The mailman's gaze flicked about unhappily. Scattered on Brady Williams's bed were dozens of envelopes, all addressed in a clear but shaky hand. Writing supplies crowded his bedside table: stamps, envelopes, a postage scale, a packet of pale-blue letterhead and a booklet of return-address stickers.

Brady's skin was pale and stretched over his jutting cheekbones. One wasted hand plucked fitfully at the edge of his blanket, while the other curled limply around a felt-tipped pen. Ink from the pen had leaked a blue spot on his linen.

As Edwina absorbed these details, she realized that some faint sound had stopped. Glancing at Williams she saw that his eyes had drifted shut. His sheet plucking slowed, then stopped.

"Harry," she said.

"I don't think — " the mailman began.

Glancing up, Harry paused with his hand inside Williams's zippered grooming kit. Grief and a look of gentle inquiry filled his eyes as Williams's chest rose and fell once, and then did not rise again.

There was a moment of silence so complete that it seemed as if all the air had been sucked from the room.

Then the mailman protested in outraged tones. "Hey, you can't just — "

A rasping intake of breath made them all jump.

"Actually," Williams said, not opening his eyes, "I can. But right now I'm just sort of practicing. Don't worry, Harry, I'll let you know when I'm really going to do it."

Harry's shoulders straightened. "I'm the doctor," he told Williams gruffly, "I'll let *you* know."

Pouring water, he thrust the glass out. "Here, have some of this. You know the drill."

Brady drank. "Now, watch," commanded Harry, but the mailman still stared at Brady Williams.

"How old are you?" Porter demanded. "And how come you write all those letters?"

A smile twitched on Williams's lips. "Twenty-nine. And they write to me. Other guys, their families if the guys can't. When they can't," he amended. "Only polite on my part to answer 'em. Wouldn't you say?"

The mailman frowned, considering this. Then his head jerked around as Harry slurped water from Williams's glass, smacking his lips with feigned relish while combing his hair with the small plastic comb from Williams's grooming kit.

"See?" Harry snarled. "See how scared I am? And I know *everything* about this disease."

Then, having neatened the few top strands he possessed, dragging the comb through his eyebrows for good measure, he plucked up Williams's toothbrush and dunked it in a cup of his mouthwash.

"Hey," said the mailman, too late. Grinning savagely, Harry began scrubbing Brady Williams's toothbrush over his own teeth.

"Brusha-brusha," he grated through the mouthwash foam. Dropping the toothbrush he began grabbing envelopes from Brady Williams's bed, stuffing them down the collar of his baggy green scrub shirt.

"Right against my body, up against my bare skin, see? Do you *see,* damn it?"

The mailman glanced around, apparently hoping that this was some mistake and he would be rescued from this crazy person. When no rescuer appeared, he let out a sigh that fogged his plastic goggles.

"Yeah, I get it," he conceded.

"But," he turned to Williams, "I still think you're a jerk, getting yourself in this fix. I mean — "

He waved a gloved hand at the calendar fixed to Williams's wall. This month's illustration was of a very lovely young fellow wearing a single very negligible item of underclothing.

"Didn't know it was a fix then, did I?" Williams smiled wanly, lifting one hand and letting it fall. "But, that's ok, I still think you're a jerk, too."

The mailman drew a circle on the floor with the toe of his shoe. "Yeah," he said finally, "well, just so we understand each other."

"And," Williams added softly, defiantly, "I'd do it again. Different, sure. But . . . all over again." His eyes fell shut.

Edwina stared. *All over again.*

Harry stuffed the last envelope into his scrub shirt and stomped out. Blinking, the mailman turned after him.

"Hey," he called. Pulling off his goggles he hurried out, shoe covers sliding and long gown flapping as he went.

"Hey, you come back here. You can't take that mail — that's federal property there! You give that back to me!"

"Is there," Edwina asked Williams, "anything I can get for you, or do for you, before I go?"

Williams chuckled. "A clean glass and toothbrush, if it's no trouble. My stuff has Harry's germs all over it now."

"Harry," Edwina said across the nursing desk a few moments later, "correct me if I'm wrong, but in the case we discussed earlier — "

"Two sets of parents," Harry said, not looking up from his scribbling, "claiming one little girl. That's the meat of the matter, isn't it?"

"Yes," she said. "And the thing is, assuming both sets of parents really do want the child,

71

which I think is true, then there's only one reason to destroy the results of those tests, or try to — isn't that right?"

Harry nodded, his pen continuing to move across the final chart. "To conceal the biology. In an argument of this sort the only side with a motive to suppress test results is the side that knows it's going to be proven wrong."

"Oh, dear," Edwina said, troubled. "That's what I thought, too. Which is awkward, because — "

"Although," Harry scribbled faster, coming to the end of his note, "I don't quite see the point there, either."

"Exactly. Because those tests are only going to be done all over again, and then it will be obvious, won't it? Not just the results, but who had a motive for getting rid of them. Which is what makes me wonder if someone's been awfully stupid?

"Or," she added slowly, "awfully smart."

At eight in the evening, the hospital's main cafeteria was crowded with the end-of-visiting-hours rush: family groups conferring over how well or poorly the patient had appeared, stunned-looking new fathers with cameras slung around their necks, and in the corner a single elderly man — they were always men — carefully shaven, dapperly dressed, eating a cup of soup with deliberate slowness.

"No," said Edwina, "it's not quite like DNA fingerprinting. The result is somewhat the same, but the technique is different."

She pulled out a small spiral notebook. "In what's called DNA fingerprinting, you see, you take X-rays of the patterns that bits of chromosomes form when they're broken up in a special way — chopped to bits with an enzyme that breaks them up, actually, at spots that are predictable.

"Then," she opened the notebook, "once you have the X-ray photographs, if you have unidentified blood or other human tissue, you can do the same to them and compare the result with pictures of known samples to see whose matches them."

"Not necessarily living samples," McIntyre ventured. "It could be a dried scraping or a swab that's been stored, for the DNA finger-prints."

"Exactly." She glanced at him approvingly. "You've been doing your homework. In tissue typing, by contrast, the living cells react in vitro — literally, in glass — with proteins from other living cells, the ones the body uses to tell self from not self."

"So DNA fingerprints show you how things look on film, but tissue typing shows what they really do. Live action."

Edwina nodded. "Listen, though — if it's not too tactless of me to ask. The thing is, I'd have thought you'd know even more of all this already. Don't police detectives get classes, or in-services, or something?"

Having assisted Harry Lemon in the solution of his problem, she had felt free to request further help on her own task. Now with McIntyre across from her at the table, she was reproducing the diagram Harry had drawn for her, meanwhile striving to remember all that he had said.

To begin, she wrote two rows of letter-and-number pairs:

A1,2; B8,44; CW4,X; DR3,4

A2,24; B35,W60; CW1,W3; DR1,2

Each row represented the antigen pairs — in real life, the antigens occurred in pairs — of a hypothetical parent.

"I mean," she told McIntyre, who was watching carefully as she wrote, "now that they're catching criminals by DNA match — "

Using the side of her beeper for a straight-edge she began drawing crossed lines between letters in the first set of pairs, connecting them to the letter pairs of the second set:

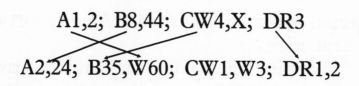

A1,2; B8,44; CW4,X; DR3

A2,24; B35,W60; CW1,W3; DR1,2

McIntyre shook his head. "I've got a general idea of what it's about, but not the fine details. Haven't needed them — for one thing we haven't made a case on DNA in this state yet."

He frowned at the diagram. "The district attorneys don't much want to, either. Evidence from new techniques is hard to take to court until there's solid precedent. And it doesn't change the rules of evidence handling any — lab people get the stuff from a scene, handle it. All I do is ask questions, think about the answers. Not," he finished self-deprecatingly, "much science to that."

"More of an art," she said, not looking up from her careful drawing, which now looked like this:

A1,2; B8,44; CW4,X; DR3,4

A2,24; B35,W60; CW1,W3; DR1,2

produces

A1,W60; B8,A2; CW4,B35; DR3,DR1

"Yes." He studied the diagram, sounding

pleased and a bit surprised. "An art, sort of. Is that it?"

"That's it." She pointed to the top two rows of letter pairs. "These are the antigens a child could inherit from these two parents. The bottom row is one possible combination.

"Which," she added, "is how they'll find out which parents belong to Hallie Dietz — by seeing whose antigens make up the pool her antigens could come from."

"Looks simple enough," he observed.

"It is, actually. Simple to do, at any rate, although not simple to develop. World War II got it going. So many burns from bombs and all, they needed a way to get skin grafts to take between unrelated people. Didn't find it, but while they were looking they found immunology, which means every transplant in the world came out of the blitz, in a way."

He nodded thoughtfully. "So I can thank Hitler for my heart transplant? Good Lord, I'm glad I don't have to decide on one right this minute then. Funny how things turn out, isn't it?"

Studying the drawing, he fell silent. Edwina, glad of a quiet moment, drank her coffee. She had spent the late afternoon in meetings: first with head nurses, whom she had entreated not to spread rumors about the murder or allow them to be spread.

Staffing shortages, she told them, were not best remedied by the panicky departure of any patient who could walk, hop on crutches, or roll down a wheelchair ramp against medical advice, which was just what would happen if a lot of silly "killer in the hospital" stories started spreading.

The head nurses hadn't been sure about the silliness of the stories, though, so Edwina's next stop had been at Chelsea's office of security affairs.

She didn't know how much good extra guards on the night shift could do, since Chelsea's security officers seemed to be of three essential types: men who remembered very clearly and bitterly the unfair reasons why they hadn't been let into the regular police academy; men who remembered with equal clarity and bitterness the even more unfair reasons why they had been kicked out of it; and men in whom memory and clarity had been pretty well abolished by drink, age, or both.

Still, having made her own share of solitary rounds down dark hallways armed only with flashlight and clipboard, she asked for and was granted the extra patrols. After that she greeted her replacement on the three-to-eleven supervisory staff: a young nurse named Ginger who was so happy at being promoted — and at getting off the night shift — that she practically fell down and kissed Edwina's feet.

By the time Ginger had been oriented to the evening shift routine and introduced to the ward personnel, it was after seven, which was when Edwina's beeper went off.

Grace Savarin had been transferred out of the recovery room and was now being admitted to the neurosurgical unit.

It was the news she had been waiting for, yet upon hearing it she found herself oddly reluctant to go and see Grace. Instead she had come to the cafeteria, lingering over the sandwiches before picking one she didn't want. At the sight of McIntyre eating his dinner alone she had felt unaccountably relieved.

"I wonder," she said now, "if someone really was after the lab tech and only took the tissue material to make it look as if — "

He shook his head as he chewed a bite of bacon cheeseburger. His first name was Martin, she had learned, and to her surprise he didn't seem to mind discussing his work with her. On the contrary, he seemed quite interested in things she had to say, listening in a calm, polite way she found reassuring and — under other circumstances — even attractive.

"No," he said when he had dealt with the bite of sandwich, "the lab tech wasn't anyone to kill. Lived alone, very quiet and bookish

— no boyfriend, no close relatives. Not a lot of money, but enough. She was going to buy a new car."

He sipped from his soft drink. "No one to notice she's gone except in her department, where I gather she'll be sorely missed. Only a bachelor's in biology, but her director had pulled a few strings to get her promoted. That was the only unusual thing about her, it seems — her skill in the lab."

Very unusual, Edwina thought; Helene Motavalli must have been something special. The others in the department would be research MDs or postdocs on fellowships, trying to get their theses done, or get grants, or be made heads of their own labs. She felt a rush of anger for whoever had thought Helene unimportant enough to kill.

"In that case," she said, "there's something missing."

His answering glance was acute, and she thought at once that this idea had occurred to him also.

"Because," she went on, "it's assumed that both the Claymores and the Dietzes believe they're in the right — that both sides think they're the child's true biological parents. But if blocking the blood tests was the motive — well. You have to know something before you can want to hide it."

He nodded. "But?"

"But," she agreed. "The Dietzes and the Claymores are the only ones — as far as we know — who care how it all comes out. And even though the Claymores have been pushing for the tests, I must confess that for me it doesn't rule them out as — "

McIntyre nodded again, more firmly.

"Meanwhile," she went on, "the blood work will be run again, so killing someone to stop it was pointless — and incriminating, eventually. Which, unless I'm sorely mistaken, means something else must be going on here."

"Very nice." He wiped his lips and crumpled his napkin on his plate. "But murderers don't always think things through the way you just did. The very act of murder, in fact, implies a kind of desperation that blocks clear thinking, wouldn't you say?"

"You mean I'm calmer than the average killer?"

"Something like that," he agreed, returning her smile. "But there's another point, too. See, if I'd done it — but I had an alibi — I might not care who thought what about my motive, right?"

Edwina stared at him; there were four of them, of course. "They're all covering for each other."

"You got it. Margaret Dietz says she and

her husband spent the afternoon walking out-doors, trying to stay calm, not stopping in any-where, and Oliver Dietz says the same."

He finished his soft drink. "Bill Claymore says he and his wife were in their hotel room having a nap, which is how she tells it, too. There's a big science-fiction convention in the Ramada Inn this week, no one noticed them one way or the other."

Edwina frowned. "Somehow I can't quite see Bill Claymore napping, can you?"

"Or Jane, either," he agreed, "but that's what they say. Meanwhile, the Dietzes left the little girl in a play group here, didn't pick her up until four-thirty when the children fin-ished watching a film on polar bears. She can't say where anyone was."

"Really," commented Edwina. "That's odd. If I had a child in this situation, I'd be keeping her near me to reassure her and myself. In-stead, it's as if they wanted her out of the way."

"Right, I asked about that. Dietz said they didn't want to seem clinging or worried, and as she doesn't get much chance to be with other children anyway, they just thought that was best."

"All of which means," she mused, "that even knowing who's lying about the child might not be enough — if someone is. What

81

about a gun? Do they have any? And can't you find out if people have fired guns recently by soot in their skin or something?"

He peered at her. "Have you heard of the Constitution? It says people have these things called rights I'm not allowed to trample on. Damned inconvenient, but I can't just check folks at random for carbon particles. I have to arrest them first, or they have to volunteer. Which they haven't."

Edwina felt chastened. "I've worked in hospitals too long. We don't even ask, we just tell people what we're going to do to them. Half the time they're lucky if we remember that much."

"Yeah, well, try that in criminal law sometime," he said. "You'll get a shock. Meanwhile, if I find out someone's lying about Hallie, I might have an idea who's lying about yesterday. But for all I know, the killer could just as easily be some maniac firing a gun off at random who took the lab stuff for some screwball reason we'd never understand."

"I suppose it could be that."

It was, in fact, pretty much what the head nurses thought: that the world was getting fuller of crazies and emptier of common sense, so that people not planning to blow the wits out of other people had to go around glancing over their shoulders all the time.

For fear, she thought sadly, of little men.

They carried their trays toward the dish room; from within it came the roar of huge dishwashing machines and the smell of bleach. "Where are you going now?" McIntyre asked.

She set her plate on the moving rubber belt and added her tray to the stack. "To see Grace Savarin. She's been out of the recovery room for an hour — they ought to have her settled by now, I think."

Which did not at all explain why she hadn't gone up at once, she thought guiltily. Stepping into the elevator beside her he seemed to understand, although of course he was trained to notice such things. Perhaps she didn't look quite as foolishly reluctant as she felt.

Idiot, she scolded herself as the car went up. Grace would look no different from any other patient, which of course was just what she found so troublesome, because Grace was different. Grace was special, and her friend. Still, she wasn't sure how to take McIntyre's unspoken offer of support.

"You know," she began, "I've been a nurse for some years now, and I do assure you — "

"Right," he said, "I've been a homicide cop for a few years, too, but that doesn't mean I'm used to it. Besides," he added as the doors opened and they stepped out, "it's different when it's one of your own."

Glancing up, she found his face taut with some private pain; it made her decide finally, to let him come along, wondering as she did so why it was always so much easier being kind to other people than letting them be kind to oneself.

But after passing through the green double doors marked Surgical Intensive Care she found herself glad of her decision, because McIntyre was right: it was different — very different — when it was one of your own.

FIVE

Chelsea Memorial's neurosurgical intensive care unit was a curving corridor lined on one side by twelve single-bed cubicles and on the other by a long, fluorescent-lit nursing desk.

Behind the desk stretched banks of monitors: EEG, EKG, and closed-circuit TV for observing patients on continuous seizure precautions. Beyond the desk were the medication rooms, a conference room used for charting and for giving reports, and a small galley kitchen.

Edwina could without hesitation have listed the contents of the medication-room cabinets, both locked and unlocked, down to the last phenobarbital tablet and morphine syringe. She knew where to find eye drops, aspirin, anti-embolism stockings, or the sort of very fine suture material that might in a pinch be used for dental floss.

She even knew what was in the refrigerator of the tiny kitchen: institutional-size cans of orange and grape juice, quarts of milk, and cans of ginger ale. Stuffed behind these was usually a paper bag labeled Do Not Steal This

Lunch — empty or full depending on how hungry the surgical resident had been the night before.

In the drawers were tea bags, bouillon cubes, pound sacks of coffee, packets of graham crackers and saltines; on the counter stood the inevitable plastic tub of peanut butter, its lid off and a plastic knife stuck into the contents.

But all this store of familiar information seemed snatched away at the sight of Grace Savarin: bathed in the eerie glow of the vital-signs monitors, motionless except for the respirator-driven rise and fall of her rib cage. There was a white plastic tube protruding from her windpipe, a slim gastric catheter taped to the side of her nose, and — so it seemed — enough wiring for a nuclear attack submarine bristling from her body.

Also, there was a spike sticking out of her skull.

Well, not a spike exactly; an intracranial pressure monitor was more like a pop-off valve. You could vent it, turning the small clear plastic three-way connector so the transducer chamber communicated with a 250-cc collection bag.

Or you could not vent it, in which case the pressure in the skull would go on rising until it squeezed the lights out of the person in there.

A pale drop of spinal fluid rose up into the venting chamber and flowed down the collection tube. Overhead, digital readouts in radium green showed blood pressure, cardiac output, end-tidal carbon dioxide, and central venous pressure. Waveform displays traced cardiac complexes and the threadlike, inscrutable bursts of brain activity on the electroencephalograph; IV bags ranged out on skyhooks dripped dextrose in normal saline, their volutrols metering constant infusions of Kefzol and Decadron.

Grace's left eye was puffed, the lid taped down loosely to protect the cornea. A few inches above it, the incision was horseshoe shaped, closed with stitches of black 4-0 surgical silk and glistening with Neosporin ointment.

Calmly Edwina took a gauze pad, moistened it, and swabbed a pale drop of fluid out of Grace's left ear. She knew it was pointless; the fluid would only collect again. Still, it was perfectly obvious that her hands must do something.

Just then Grace's own nurse came in bearing several filled syringes. Edwina stepped back from the bed. "Sorry, I don't mean to meddle, I just — "

Grace's nurse was new and quite young; doubtfully, Edwina took in her bleached hair, reddened cheeks, and eyes gummy as paint pots with cosmetics.

The quick comprehending smile redeemed all, however. "It really does make you want to do something, doesn't it? Like wave your magic wand or something."

"Yes," Edwina said, "that's just what it makes me want to do. Has any of her family been in?"

Shaking her head, the nurse shot one of the syringes into the port of an IV bag. "No, we've been wondering about that," she said with a questioning glance at Edwina.

In the glow of the monitors Edwina's skin was pale bluish white, while Grace's was dark, almost truly black. "I guess they're not likely to visit." Edwina swallowed hard.

McIntyre moved toward the door. "We haven't been able to get in touch with the family, either," he said when she had followed him there. "You know any reason why?"

Of course they haven't, she thought angrily. "The mother is dead," she recited, "the father is disabled and alcoholic. The fifteen-year-old sister has two small kids and is expecting a third. There's a brother who's older, but I don't know what he does. Any of them could be anywhere."

Her remark about the brother was not quite a lie. James Savarin made it his business to keep people from knowing what he did, as failure in this regard would no doubt bring him quite a long prison term.

"They all live," she added, "in a tenement on Oak Street. Grace gets the welfare checks from her father, unless he's cashed them and spent them, and pays the bills. Otherwise they'd all be out on the street — which they will be soon, without her."

McIntyre sighed. "All these little people that people kill, or try to. Funny how important a lot of them turn out to be."

His pocket pager gave out a tweet; glancing around, he spied a telephone on the nursing desk and headed for it.

Back in Grace's cubicle the nurse was drawing a sample from the arterial line, flushing the tubing with heparin and clearing it before screwing on a glass syringe.

Bright red blood sprang into the tubing; good color, Edwina thought automatically, then thought again that none of this made any sense.

"That was Talbot," McIntyre said when he returned, his voice grim. "The little girl is missing."

Grace's nurse looked up. "How awful. My nephew was missing in the mall a whole day once. My sister nearly went crazy before he showed up."

"Yes, it is awful," Edwina said slowly, and yet it began to explain a great deal. After all, if the child couldn't be found, she couldn't be retested, could she?

A glance at McIntyre's face showed that his thoughts mirrored her own.

"Oh, my," she said as a new and worse fear made a lump in her throat. Once lodged, it would move neither up nor down, sticking instead like a pill too large and bitter to swallow.

Half an hour later as she closed her apartment door behind her she heard a faint questioning *mrupp?* followed by a thump and the clicking of claws on polished hardwood.

In a moment Maxie appeared on the foyer tiles, yawning exaggeratedly to show he hadn't missed her in the slightest. When she lifted the cat he butted his black-velvet head against her chin and squirmed at once to be let down again.

"Just a fool for love, huh Max?" Still, it was good to see the beast.

Leaving him to sniff uninterestedly at her duffel bag, she went through the pantry to the kitchen, where she took out a cut-crystal highball glass and filled it with a businesslike mixture of Scotch and ice. This she carried to the living room, snapping on lamps as she went, comforted as always by the sight of her own things in their own places.

The maroon leather club chairs faced one another across the low inlaid chess table, upon whose spruce and rosewood surface stood the ivory chess warriors her great-grandfather had brought back from one of his China trips. On the hearth lay the brass andirons from the summer house in Newport, topped by three large fragrant cedar logs awaiting the touch of the Cape Cod lighter.

Above hung the gilt-framed oil of her father, E. R. Crusoe. The portraitist had given his long, stern face a judicious look befitting the industrialist, diplomat, and smoother of the way to foreign markets for administrations from Roosevelt to Kennedy and beyond.

Not for the first time, Edwina wondered how her father would have approached the situation she now faced. Also not for the first time, he failed to enlighten her, preferring as he had in life to let her find her own way through such mazes.

Mewing theatrically, Maxie leapt to the back of a club chair and teetered there, then sprang to the piano to dance out a garbled version of "Kitten on the Keys" before streaking away down the hall.

Sighing, Edwina closed the piano lid. Over on the little cherry desk, the answering machine blinked; quickly she zipped through the week's worth of messages waiting there, filing them away in her mind to be dealt with in the morning.

As she did, the phone gave out a low whirr much like the warning of a rattlesnake. Edwina regarded the instrument glumly, for at this hour there was only one person likely to be calling.

"Hello, darling," came Harriet Crusoe's voice the moment she heard the receiver lifting. "I tried earlier, but I suppose you were off playing handmaiden to the doctors again."

"Mother," Edwina began, "it's not playing. It's work, and I do wish that just for once you could — "

But of course her mother could not. Occupations approved of by Harriet for ladies included the showing of small, unpleasantly inbred dogs, the daubing of small, unpleasantly imitative watercolors, and the playing of golf games at country clubs so exclusive as to be practically fossilized. That Harriet herself pursued none of these occupations did not, apparently, signify.

"And I don't suppose you've met any nice young doctors at that hospital of yours?" she inquired pointedly.

Which, as she very well knew, was pushing her luck. By nice she meant marriageable:

properly ancestored, decently reared, and if possible generously financed — although the last was not an absolute requirement.

"No, Mother," Edwina said, just as she had said a hundred or more times before.

Then, because she knew Harriet hadn't called to ask this or any other of her numerous intrusive and impertinent questions, she let herself relax into the simple pleasure of her mother's voice.

How lucky I am, she thought, that Harriet has lived long enough for me to stop hating her.

She had spent much of her early life feeling guilty over her advantages — and, unreasonably, blaming Harriet for them. Being rich, pretty, and intelligent as a child, it had not escaped her that many of her schoolmates were homely, dull, impoverished, or all three.

That such unfortunate qualities were also noticed by their owners, especially as they compared themselves to Edwina, only deepened her unhappiness. Her skin became a torment to her as she prayed without success for the slightest blemish. Her body, always coltish and athletic, lengthened without widening no matter what or how much food she managed to stuff into it.

As for her mind, there was nothing she could do about that: it was there, like a scar or a birthmark. Thus she grew resigned to the sparkling reports of her schoolmistresses, even while turning in yet another perfect outline, essay, or — most lamentable of all — multiple-choice examination.

Intelligence, the young Edwina had thought sadly, was like being able to play the piano at parties: fun, but what did one do when the party was over? Besides, it made people afraid of her.

This state of affairs, however, did not go unpitied by her parents, each of whom had faced the same question and answered it — at length and with difficulty — in a different way.

Her father, retired to his Litchfield County farm by the time of Edwina's birth, raised his daughter and his horses by the same code: look to the horizon, and the devil take the hindmost.

Her mother, an author, viewed her child as an ongoing project like a novel, dosing her with museums, planetariums, and day trips to famous flower gardens whose green lawns had been rolled daily for hundreds of years with obvious good result.

These lessons were not lost on Edwina, who shrugged off the spots and struggles of her schoolmates unregretfully once she was relieved of their company. Being rich and pretty, after all, was not the worst burden in the world. Only it was not enough.

Awakening on the morning of her twenty-first birthday Edwina had drawn back the lavender-scented sheets and padded to her bedroom window. All around her hung the trophies of her accomplishments: riding cups, ribbons, and medals; scrolls and diplomas; faded corsages, laboriously earned; the dog-eared dance cards of the dowagers' favorite, toward whom they endlessly nudged their whey-faced, unprepossessing sons.

Edwina ignored the lot. Outside her window the sun shone slantingly down through oceans of pink-white apple blossoms. In the warm air floated smells of new-mown grass, freshly turned earth, and good rich horse manure. Perched on a branch very near — so near she could see into its beady eye — a robin chirped indomitably.

I can do anything I want, she thought; I have a decent brain and more money than anyone deserves.

Whereupon she went straight down to the state university and enrolled in the nursing program. At the time she had only the dimmest idea of what actually being a nurse might entail. From her reading and a few experiences as a visitor in hospitals, however, she was sure that when nurses woke up in the morning they didn't lie in bed, wondering what trivial amusement might be found to while away another long day. Nurses had work to do: it mattered if they did it, and it mattered if they did it well. That idea appealed intensely to Edwina. She determined to try it out at once.

Her mother insisted on seeing this as some bizarre and — one hoped — temporary aberration; her father, amused, promptly settled another million on her. Shortly thereafter he died of a stroke while riding his favorite horse; fifteen years later it still seemed to Edwina that Harriet had accepted the death of a much-loved husband more easily than the career of an only daughter.

"Anyway, darling, do come for lunch." Harriet's coaxing voice drew Edwina back into the present as it embarked upon its dearest and most perennial project: the luring of Edwina to Harriet's domain, the better to ply her there with luxuries.

Lunch would no doubt involve wine, pale yellow and smelling of flowers, along with other delicacies not often indulged in by Edwina: crepes plump with lobster morsels, glistening in lemony hollandaise. Fresh berry tart, the pastry so light it dissolved on the tongue, and coffee rich as chocolate.

Harriet named a day just wistfully enough and Edwina gave in at once, before the old lady could change her mind — an about-face of which she was quite capable, for while she inveigled her daughter by fair means and foul, America's most popular romantic-suspense novelist Harriet Crusoe was herself a steadily sought-after lunch date and not in the habit of wasting her hospitality on the unappreciative.

"The camellias are blooming on the sun porch," Harriet went on happily, "we'll sit out there, shall we? And Watkins, the old dear, has been forcing a huge fat pot of paper-whites for you, so you can take them along to the apartment when you go."

The apartment. When you go. Edwina knew she need only say the word to reenter a world filled entirely with unearned treats: winters at Marina Key, summers on the farm, and no one to be responsible for but herself.

Momentarily, she was tempted by more than a steady parade of delicious edibles, products of Harriet's French-trained, Swiss-disciplined kitchen help. But no: absence did make the heart grow fonder, especially of Harriet, from whom a solid month's separation was sometimes still required to do the trick.

"Yes, Mother," Edwina pronounced a final time before telling Harriet good-night. Then, carrying her drink, she went down the hall past the guest room and the spare room through her bedroom and into the huge marble-tiled bath — for she had decided all those years ago to be useful, not uncomfortable. She ran a tub of hot water and lavender bath salts and sank into it with an exhausted sigh.

Some working girl, she mocked herself. But if she was rich, at least she was not idly rich, and as her accountants flung wads of money at every organized charity in sight — and at some quite disorganized ones — Edwina didn't see why she shouldn't enjoy a bit of it herself.

Defiantly she poured in another large dose of bath salts, then took her first serious swallow of the Scotch and closed her eyes to think.

Angry, disgusted, and apparently deciding to finish his part in the Dietz-Claymore matter without delay, the director of the tissue-typing lab had phoned the Dietz and Claymore families at about five that evening, asking them if they could come in at once.

Oliver Dietz had requested only that the blood samples not be drawn where the shootings had occurred, as Hallie was upset about it, so they agreed to meet at the admitting desk in the lobby on the hospital's main floor.

The appointment was fixed for seven, but the Claymores arrived a little early. The lab director took them down a short hallway to the cubicle where incoming patients had routine blood work done; in this room he took the samples without any trouble and completed the necessary paperwork.

By then the Dietzes had arrived and were waiting in the lobby when Jane and William Claymore came out. No conversation was exchanged, but in the corridor behind the admitting desk the child asked her father to go first. She looked anxious, the lab director thought, so Oliver Dietz went ahead into the cubicle where his blood also was drawn without the slightest difficulty.

Upon his return, however, he found his wife calling for the child. Margaret Dietz had gone into the ladies' room. The corridor was furnished with one of these, and the child was old enough to sit outside alone for a few moments.

When she came out, though, Hallie wasn't in sight. She hadn't been seen leaving, nor had she been seen since.

Opening her eyes, Edwina found Maxie perched on the edge of the bathtub, gazing at her. Reaching out his paw he batted at the cooling bathwater.

"Oh, all right," she told him, climbing out and wrapping herself in her old terry-cloth robe. One of the keenest pleasures of solitude, she thought, was the freedom to indulge in dowdiness.

"It is a puzzle, though," she told the animal, "you have to admit that. How did she get out of the hospital? No one saw her in the lobby or the cafeteria or the hallways, and no one saw her outside."

Maxie tipped his head as if to say that when he vanished, no one ever saw him do it either. As if to prove it, the next time she looked down he was gone.

"Right," she said. "But you're a cat."

Then, reluctantly, she turned her attention to the novel lying in wait for her on the bedside table. She had been putting it off, but Harriet would surely want to know what she thought of it — as if a million dollars, instant translation into a dozen languages, and the prospect of another movie of the week weren't enough reassurance for her. Sighing, Edwina opened the volume. With its lipstick-pink cover and plot full of dark secrets, brooding heroes, and bright, unlikely tomorrows it would at least make an effective soporific.

Half an hour later, though, she revised her opinion: her mother was really very good. Smiling over the description of the plucky heroine — a young woman bearing an odd resemblance to herself who, rejecting fireside and family, went stubbornly off to become a World War II Red Cross volunteer — Edwina at last fell asleep.

Not until dawn did she open her eyes to wonder what else William Claymore might have found while he was busy hunting one little girl. After all, when you lifted a rock you often found something nasty wriggling beneath.

And William Claymore, by all accounts, had left no stone unturned in his search for Hallie Dietz.

SIX

"I said no, and I meant *no!*"

Issuing from one of the patient rooms, the old man's quavery shout was followed by what sounded unmistakably like a loaded breakfast tray being hurled against a wall.

Edwina looked up from the desk on Seven West where she was waiting for a call to be returned, meanwhile trying to make sense of two new staffing requests passed along by Julia Friedlander — just, Edwina supposed, to prepare her for what a nursing director had to put up with, day in and day out.

When no further sounds came from the corridor she returned to the memoranda. The more she read them, the more the idea of tray throwing seemed not only reasonable but even, at the moment, attractive.

The first, from Chelsea's medical chief of staff, insisted that all medical patients whose conditions were listed as serious or critical be cared for henceforth only by graduate nurses with four-year baccalaureate degrees.

A laudable ambition, Edwina thought grimly.

The second, issued by the chief of surgery, demanded that surgical patients likewise be entrusted only to the care of degreed nurses, with the additional requirement that such care be administered on a one-to-one (or, in intensive care units where patients were better monitored, one-to-two) basis.

Which was also laudable, but hospital staffing didn't depend on ambitions. It depended on human beings, each one of whom had to be found, hired, paid, and provided with holidays, vacation, insurance, sick time, and pension benefits, for a start.

Meanwhile, in a twelve-hundred-bed facility whose occupancy rate ran at about 80 percent, the memos blithely mandated recruitment of at least two hundred new graduate nurses — at a time when such creatures were so scarce as to be for all practical purposes mythical beasts — assuming there was any money in the staffing budget for them, which there was not, and assuming Edwina intended to pay the slightest bit of attention to the memos, which she did not.

Sighing, she tossed the memos in the trash, but this only brought another unpleasant item to her attention: the morning newspaper.

Custody Fight Stalled as Cops Hunt Missing Child, ran the headline.

Below, the whole business had been laid out

in tones just barely avoiding glee. To a reporter dying to write about something besides just what poison had been dumped by which corporate polluter into exactly how much of the state's drinking-water supply, the absent Hallie Dietz had probably looked like a gift from God, or at least like comic relief.

Edwina regarded the paragraphs that recapped in detail the past two days' events. Featured prominently was a photograph of Jane Claymore, in which she appeared defiant and more than a little unhinged. The hospital, Claymore maintained, had been "grossly negligent," its treatment of her and her husband lacking in ways she considered "plainly actionable."

Which probably had several hospital administrators choking over their cornflakes this morning, being as it was so obviously a direct quote from one of the Claymores' legal beagles, of which they had kennels full.

Not much better was the comment of Margaret Dietz, opining that as her daughter disappeared from Chelsea Memorial, she hoped the hospital meant to help find the child. She did not, however, suggest how this might be accomplished; perhaps she thought some high-tech gadget ordinarily used to locate tumors might be employed. Glancing at the stubbornly silent telephone, Edwina thought about how glad hospital counsel was going to be to have such good, clearheaded advice on the situation. As she did so a second crash came from the corridor, this one sounding like an IV pole going over, taking a glass IV bottle with it.

An instant later Jennifer Stedman emerged hastily from the third room on the left, looking as usual like a cross between a Botticelli angel and a Rubens nude, except of course that she wasn't nude. She was wearing a white lab coat, blue button-down shirt, white slacks, and white running shoes. Her wheat-colored hair was held back by two tortoiseshell combs, and her eyes even at a distance were the deep purple-blue of forest violets.

In short, Jennifer was the kind of girl men fought to peel grapes for, assuming they could stop their hands from shaking and their voices from breaking at the mere astonishing sight of her, but at the moment she was also a first-year medical resident. This accounted for the look on Jennifer's face: exhaustion mingled with desperation.

Slamming a chart into the chart rack, she yanked out another and slapped it open on the nursing desk. "Fine. He wants to go home, I'll send him home. Stubborn, disagreeable old man, why should I care if he loses his insurance coverage?"

From Jennifer, this was severe talk indeed. "Why," Edwina asked, "will that happen?"

Tight-lipped, Jennifer snatched up a pharmacy order sheet and scribbled on it.

"Because insurance companies are run by idiots, that's why. He needs to go to a nursing home, he's much too fragile to get along on his own and his wife is almost as bad — she comes to my clinic. She can't take care of him and he knows that, he agrees with that."

Jennifer ripped the order form apart, flung the carbon at the pharmacy message-box, and snapped the original into the open chart.

"But for his insurance to cover the nursing home, he can't just be obviously sick, he has to be officially sick. If I send him home first, he's well enough to go home, see? They'll only pay if he goes straight to the nursing home from the hospital."

She snapped the chart shut. "All he wants is one more night in his own bed with his own wife, and I can't give it to him. It isn't fair. God, I hate this."

Edwina considered. "Could you send him home, wait until he gets sick enough to be readmitted, and send him to the nursing home next time?"

Ignoring the gruesomely cynical expedience of this — for she wasn't inexperienced, only tired — Jennifer shook her head.

"Do you know how long it takes to find a vacant bed in one of those places? If he's not in it tomorrow, someone else will be. Which he won't, so I guess I'd better tell them not to hold it for him." Glumly, she reached for the phone.

"Wait," Edwina said, partly to keep the telephone clear for herself and partly because Jennifer was being hasty. "Which does your old man want most — his own bed, or his own wife? I mean," she added, "you just said yourself she's a sick woman."

"I don't — oh." Jennifer brightened. "I could admit her, couldn't I? Because if he can't go home to be with her . . . she is weak. I could say she's much weaker suddenly. But Edwina, do you think I can get away with it?"

Someday Jennifer would realize how much she really could get away with, at which point the entire male half of the population would be in deep and serious trouble — especially her husband Eric, a rising young stockbroker who was, by all reports, a ninny.

There was for instance the day Eric's colleague had suffered a heart attack at work: Eric had seized the victim's Rolodex and begun poaching clients before the ambulance guys got the stretcher out the office door. His latest bad habit was accusing Jennifer of having affairs.

"God," she'd said miserably, "I'm on thirty-six-hour call and I've got a two-year-old kid at home — the only person who'd want an affair with me would be a necrophiliac."

"Admit the old lady, Jennifer," Edwina told her now, "and if you catch any flak for it, call me."

After all, everybody else did. As if on signal, the telephone rang at last.

It was McIntyre. "What," she asked him, "if it's not about Hallie Dietz at all?"

There was a brief silence. "Then why is she gone?"

"I don't know," she admitted. "Maybe to muddy the waters. But as long as she's missing, a lot of attention stays focused on her, which might be just what someone wants."

"Huh. That's an idea, all right." McIntyre sounded less than thunderstruck. "Why don't I get hold of the depositions," he went on, "the stuff the Claymores had to give the courts in the first place. Maybe find out which private investigators they used, too. That make you happy?"

"You thought of all that already, didn't you? You were going to do that anyway."

"Talbot's over at the hall of records right now," he admitted, his smile almost audible, "and I called Claymore's private guys just to

108

rattle their cages a little bit. Who knows what they'll say if they're nervous."

"Oh. That's good, then. Sorry, I didn't mean to — "

"Forget it. I was getting ready to call you anyway, let you know your cover's blown. I figured you'd want to know."

"Cover? What's that mean, cover?" Edwina tried to sound innocent but found she had fallen out of practice.

"My boss got a call from your boss," he said, "the big boss, not your Mrs. Friedlander. Seems like there's scandal to be cleaned up and she tapped you. That about the size of it from your end?"

"Uh-huh," she said.

"Al Geberth was on the horn first thing this morning," he went on, "and the upshot is, I keep you in the picture, you keep feeding me the medical stuff."

Edwina blinked. "Geberth, Chelsea's corporate president? He wants me — I mean, he wants that?"

"Yep. And since he's also a big backstage honcho down at town hall who my boss wants kept satisfied . . . end of story. Except for one thing." His voice hardened.

"I know," she conceded unhappily. "Leave the police work to the police officers."

"No, that's not it. When I talked to you

I'd already had two guys from our labs try explaining tissue typing to me, and I didn't understand what either one of them said. From you I got it simple and I got it fast — which is why I'm putting up with this arrangement, strictly against my better judgment."

"So," she said slowly, "you want more?"

"Right. For now, the short course on liver diseases — the one Jill Claymore died of, especially."

"I can do that, but — "

"And one other thing. I'll skip the macho protective rap out of concern for your sensibilities."

Edwina grinned.

"Besides, I can already tell I might as well shout down a drainpipe as try telling you anything. So I'll say this once: you get hurt, or you mess me up in any way at all, I'm going to be annoyed. *Very* annoyed. Have you got that?"

"Got it," she said, no longer grinning, but he had already hung up.

"Liver disease," Moira Gluck said in a brusque Germanic accent.

She was tall, lean and fiftyish, wearing a long tattered lab coat over a battered tweed skirt and man-tailored shirt. "You've got a year, maybe five years, for learning about this?"

No makeup, no jewelry, no smile. No suggestion even that she possessed the facial musculature for a smile. Her office was furnished with gray metal file cabinets, a gray metal desk, and gray metal chairs.

Moira Gluck seemed to be made of gray metal, too. Stainless steel, perhaps, or some less malleable alloy.

"Or maybe just the basics, hmm? A few months only you can spare." Grimacing, she pulled an enormous leather-bound volume from a shelf and let it thump to her desk.

The Liver appeared to contain about sixteen hundred pages. Below the gold-leaf title imprinted on its spine stood the words Volume One. Moira Gluck folded her bony hands and waited.

"Sorry to have troubled you," Edwina said, having been told that the chief of the pediatric liver service was almost as fast and good a teacher as Harry Lemon but not that she was also a jerk.

"Wait. I am rude? You don't put up with it?"

Halfway out the door Edwina turned. "That's right. It seems I'm wasting your time — I'll try someone less eminent."

Gluck tapped *The Liver* in brisk summoning

fashion. "Good, sit. Maybe you even have a brain, hmm? Most of my students — paugh." She spat the syllable like a prune pit. "Tell me what you want, now, quick — and why you want it."

As Edwina did so, Gluck's look grew more thoughtful. She appeared almost human when told about Hallie Dietz's disappearance.

"So now another child suffers. Jill Claymore was my patient, did you know that?"

"No. But even if I had known, I'm not asking for confidential medical information, only — "

Moira Gluck gave a snort of derision. "The dead have no privacy, or weren't you aware? They become — horrible phrase — interesting cases, and we give them immortality in the journals. To be an interesting case is to die fast, if one is fortunate, but to be forgotten only slowly."

"And Jill Claymore was interesting?"

Gluck nodded. "I have written already three papers about her." She thrust a stack of journals across the desk. "The data are here on what she had — alpha-trypsin deficiency. Mostly it makes lung death in young adults with no reason to expect such a thing. Sometimes it kills kids by wrecking their livers."

She opened a journal to a graph. "The death rate peaks at age three, then flattens out, you see? Because most kids with the syndrome die before then. Without liver transplant it is a death sentence, a fatal diagnosis."

"But," Edwina frowned at the graph, "Jill Claymore lived to be much older."

Moira Gluck nodded grimly. "Longer than any other child reported with the illness. Also, in her it did not appear until late. She was never healthy, but this disease appears almost at birth in most children who inherit the trait."

"Inherit? It's genetic?"

Gluck opened another of the journals to a set of drawings. "Yes. See here, the spiral strands represent the chromosomes, made from nucleic acids. Groups of nucleic acids are genes — the instructions that say how the body should make proteins. If any mistakes are in the instructions, the proteins are made wrong, or not at all. That is what causes all genetic diseases. For this one you need mistakes in some paired genes, called alleles."

She sat back. "So the disease is autosomal recessive — it means both parents must have the trait for the child to get sick. And even then it is only a one-in-four chance the child will get both damaged genes of the pair."

"Can you test for it?" Edwina asked. "To see if a person is a carrier?" Because if you could, you might find both Dietzes carried the damaged gene, or both Claymores. That wouldn't prove the carriers had produced Jill, but it would be suggestive.

"Yes," Gluck said, "sometimes. But the blood test is not always diagnostic. Simpler just to look at the family. That was another reason Jill was interesting, you see."

"You tested. And no family history of liver disease."

"Correct. It was confusing at the time. Mutation in the Pi alleles — the genes that cause this — is rare. But when we tissue typed her family — she needed a kidney too, by then, and we hoped to find one quickly — the explanation appeared."

"The Claymores weren't really her family."

"Not in the blood sense. They were shocked. And angry."

"They're still angry," Edwina said.

Gluck closed the journals and drew them back across the desk. "Me, too. Jill was a lovely child, at first. Not so lovely at the end. If we'd had relatives to search among, we might have found a kidney for her, maybe even kept her alive long enough to find a liver. Instead . . ." She shrugged. "We can't win them all, hmm? Still, I should like someday to meet the person who began this confusion in the first place. To describe what was the last week of Jill Claymore's life to them, in precise detail. It would be not near enough punishment, I think, but it would be a start."

"The clinic director who's supposed to have switched them is dead, you know," Edwina said. "He hung himself just before his trial."

"Of course, I had forgotten." Moira Gluck nodded slowly. "So sad," she said, not sounding at all as if she thought it was.

James Lobrutto wasn't the only atheist Edwina knew, but he was the only one who was also a Roman Catholic priest.

"Edwina," he greeted her as she departed Moira Gluck's office, "what's this I've been hearing? You changing careers at this late date?"

Falling into step beside him, she thought again that he was too good-looking for a cleric. With strong, even features, curly hair, and deep brown eyes that could only be described as dreamy, he looked more like a heartthrob movie star.

"Priests aren't supposed to listen to gossip," she scolded him, "and I'm not changing careers. I'm just a walking medical dictionary for the police, is all, in case they need one."

Lobrutto looked wise. "Right. If I know you, you'll be marching the culprit out of here at the point of a scalpel before I can say carotid endarterectomy. Or," he added seriously, "I hope you will. Some of the kids are scared."

He spent most of his free time on the adolescent ward where he played endless Nintendo games, watched music videos by the hour, and drank so much Diet Pepsi he ought to have sloshed when he walked. Meanwhile, he quietly went on doing what he did best: listening to the kids and being adored by them for it.

"I'd have thought they'd be too old to be worried," she told him, "or too cool to admit they were."

He shook his head, troubled. "They've been asking a lot of questions — like why their doors don't have locks. As if it were a privacy issue, you know, but it's not. One boy has a .22 at home, wanted to bring it in. For protection, he said."

"Uh-oh. Maybe I'll ask security to up their visibility on your ward too for a few days, until things straighten out."

"I'd appreciate it. Meanwhile, I've got another problem I wish I knew what to do about."

From the ward social room they were approaching came laughter, loud music, and sounds of the horseplay all but the sickest or most immobilized young patients thrived on.

Just outside this room sat a young girl, her wheelchair surrounded by a forest of IV poles. Beside her stood an oxygen tank in a small wheeled cart.

"Gina Krill," Lobrutto said softly. "Cystic fibrosis."

The girl's sticklike arms were implacably folded on her chest. Clapped to her mouth was a clear plastic oxygen mask at which she sucked rhythmically and determinedly.

"If she weren't sick," Lobrutto said, "she'd be rehearsing the lead in her school play. But she caught cold, it turned into pneumonia, and she had to come in here. So she's lost the part. Probably she won't be alive for next year's play . . . and she knows it. And I have no idea what to say to her."

The look on his face reminded Edwina of the day he'd had his faith blitzed out of him, years earlier in the emergency room where she had been a staff nurse. The busload of schoolkids had been no match for a highballing eighteen-wheeler; the horrified young priest had run out of holy oil and done the last half-dozen anointings with pharmaceutical glycerin before it was all over.

Down the hall now, Gina Krill picked peevishly at the tape on her IV site.

"Heck," Lobrutto said, squaring his shoulders. "It's not the thought that counts, is it? It's the action that counts — I hope." He headed for the girl, whose sad, thin face brightened at the sight of him.

* ★ ★

It's the action that counts, Edwina told herself firmly as Oliver Dietz upset his coffee cup. He had caught her on her way to the medical library and begged her to sit down with him.

"Here," she said, handing him her napkin, and watching him mop ineffectually at his loud plaid jacket. With his round, ruddy cheeks and flaming hair, his hands herky-jerky as if yanked by invisible strings, he really did resemble Howdy Doody.

He glanced up and caught her watching him. "G-good thing Hallie got her mother's looks, I g-guess."

"I was thinking you must be terribly upset," she lied.

His laugh was a bleat of despair. "The police think we're huh-hiding Hallie. They think I m-might have — "

He stopped, ran trembling fingers over his face. "I'm not that kind of man. I feel like I've wuh-walked into a nightmare and I cuh-can't wake up."

"I'm sure the police are doing all they can to find her. You'll have her back soon."

"Will we? She's out of our custody now. Wuh-what if the Claymores have sent her to Europe, or . . . Bill Claymore has a lot of money, you know. That's how this has muh-managed to get so far — and because we're

118

not the court's idea of t-traditional parents."

He sighed, shook his head. "I nuh-know how I seem to people. A funny-looking, suh-stuttering little wimp."

She stared, stricken. Oliver Dietz was just about the most ineffective-seeming person she had ever met in her life, and the eyes behind his thick glasses told her not to bother denying it.

"With," he added relentlessly, "a big strong wife. We're like a cartoon. Only not to ourselves. M-my wife loves me, and my little girl thinks I'm a hero. We were huh-happy."

He pulled out his wallet and thrust snapshots across the table: Maggie Dietz in a white wedding dress embroidered in flowers and flowing to her bare feet, Dietz beside her in white shirt, blue jeans, and leather sandals. Behind them loomed an old Volkswagen bus, its sides emblazoned with peace symbols.

The final snapshots were of Hallie: as an infant, a toddler in rompers, and as a breathtakingly pretty little girl in sneakers, jeans, and a sweatshirt. Dietz had caught her flying downhill on her bicycle, a grin of excitement mingled with alarm on her pixie face.

"She's lovely," Edwina said. "It's hard to see what could have been wrong with your parenting, looking at that."

"W-we tried for five years to h-have her,"

he said. "W-we thought it was hopeless, and then . . ."

He shrugged, nearly upsetting his coffee cup again. "B-but Claymore made us sound perverse. See, I do most of the mothering things, always have. That's why Maggie and I work out so well — we never tried to force each other into any ruh-roles. And the farm, it's pretty isolated, and with Hallie not going to school — "

"I understand. The Claymores had an argument to give the court. Blood kinship *and* the best interests of the child."

He nodded miserably. "They're so normal and puh-prosperous. And they just won't give up."

"But," Edwina said, "when Hallie does turn up and the blood tests can finally be completed . . ."

Dietz sighed. "We still don't know all about that clinic. I'm sure Hallie's ours, but what — just what if — I'm wrong?

"Well," he put out his hand, which was icy cold, "thanks. Maggie's so upset, and I guess I just needed someone to talk to. But I'd better get back in case anything huh-happens."

Watching him fumble his way out of the cafeteria she thought that under the best of circumstances he was not a man who much enjoyed conversation.

120

Uncomfortable with strangers and afflicted with a speech impediment that must have made every syllable an effort, even painful — still, raising a child was no job for a weakling, and he had apparently been quite excellent at this task.

Nor had his meeting her this morning been accidental, she felt sure; he had come here on purpose to face a chore he found difficult — to give, perhaps, precisely the impression he had.

A worried man with no clue about where his daughter was, a man too clumsy even to handle a cup of coffee safely, much less be an accurate pistol shot or planner of complicated schemes.

An innocent man: it was a portrait Oliver Dietz might very well want to present, she thought, especially if it weren't true.

Meanwhile it was now nearly noon, and the medical library still hadn't been visited; downing the last of her coffee Edwina left the cafeteria and had gotten nearly to the lobby doors when she heard the overhead page operator pronouncing her name.

Loudly, repeatedly, and urgently.

"What's up?"

The secretary in the intensive-care unit aimed a long red-varnished nail at Grace

121

Savarin's cubicle. "I'm not sure, but Miss Waldrop wanted you."

Ellen Waldrop's small, plump figure managed somehow to seem bustling even when she was standing still — her gray-brown curls bobbing, her fingers fluttering, her lip perpetually caught her teeth as she worried lest she make some mistake.

She had made one once: a medication error that nearly killed the two-year-old whose IV she'd mistakenly flushed with potassium chloride. It was the kind of rare, unfortunate mishap nurses dreaded, and although based on the circumstances she was not held negligent, Ellen had never really recovered from it.

Now she hurried to the cubicle doorway, her glance darting shyly and her small pudgy hands pressed together humbly. "Oh, I'm so sorry to bother you, Miss Crusoe. Actually I'd have called sooner, only the doctors were here then, and — "

"Trouble?" Grace's room seemed in good order: monitors tracing, IV solutions dripping, and the respirator settings all correct. Nothing was wrong with Ellen's nursing skills; only her flustered mannerisms made it seem as if there might be.

"Well," Ellen said, "first the neurology service came by and I told them about the blood in the endotracheal tube."

Stepping to the side of the bed, Edwina frowned at the tube protruding from the corner of Grace's mouth. There was a darkish streak inside it; in the wastebasket by the bed lay several used suction catheters, all of them heavily stained.

"And they said it was a hard intubation. In the emergency room, you know, and the blood was just a little oozing from that. They told me I shouldn't be such a . . . such a nervous Nellie." She winced, feeling the jab afresh. "I don't think I'm a nervous Nellie, Miss Crusoe. I think it was a reasonable question."

"Yes," said Edwina. There really was quite a lot of blood. "And then what happened?"

Ellen clasped and unclasped her hands. "Well, they left and then the surgical people came by. So I told them the same thing, that I didn't think it was right and would they take a look."

"And?" The stain inside the tube darkened, climbing several centimeters. Respirator alarms shrilled briefly and quieted.

"They said keep an eye on it and let them know if it didn't clear or if it got worse. But they didn't seem concerned about it, either. And I know — "

Another dark bolus rose in the tube, then slid back.

" — you wanted to hear all that happened with Miss Savarin," Ellen went on. "And besides — well. If anything goes wrong, I know who'll be the goat. Not," she finished resentfully, "any of them. They'll try to make it look like my fault."

A second shrill of protest came from the respirator. "Tell you what," Edwina said, "let's lavage the tube with a few squirts of saline, clean her out real well, and see how she looks then."

Probably the neurologists and surgeons were right: getting an endotracheal tube into a trauma patient was not a genteel procedure. Racing to get an airway opened up, an anesthesiologist might cut a patient's mouth, scrape the throat, maybe even loosen a tooth.

They had little choice: if you didn't have an airway, you didn't have a patient. Later, though, even a few streaks of blood could look like a lot.

Hands gloved, Edwina waited while Ellen shot a syringeful of saline down the tube, threaded the suction catheter down after it, and closed the port with a fingertip.

Streaked saline shot up into the catheter. "Not too bad," Edwina commented. "Let's just go down one more time."

"OK," Ellen said, "I think that will — oh my god."

Bright red blood flooded the suction tube. Edwina closed the port, but the tube didn't clear.

More blood shot up — lots more.

"Get the code cart in here, please," Edwina said, "and get anesthesia and surgery up here. Now — super-stat."

This wasn't oozing and this wasn't streaking; this was hemorrhaging, a big arterial pumper that would keep right on pumping as long as it had a blood pressure behind it.

Which at this rate wouldn't be for long.

Ellen grabbed a liter bottle of saline, thrust it at Edwina, and headed for the door, her funny toddling gait changed abruptly to a purposeful stride as if this sudden emergency had at last cleared her mental switches.

During Ellen's absence Edwina alternated between suctioning up blood and trying to force oxygen down the tube. Behind her, the respirator shrilled its eardrum-puncturing disconnect alarm, the blood-pressure monitor began whining dissonantly, and the EKG recorder spewed a paper trail of Grace's deteriorating cardiac complexes.

Squeezing the resuscitator bag with one hand she pressed the bed controls with the other to get Grace's feet up, then reversed her decision and put them down again. Routing blood to Grace's head would send oxygen to her brain, which by now was surely in dire need of it, but it would also fill up the ruptured artery.

Probably the innominate artery, so vulnerably near the surface of the trachea and possibly scraped or bruised as the tube was going in. It was nearly unheard of, but it was what had happened; by the amount of blood it had to be what had happened.

Which meant there was no way out of this; even as her hands kept squeezing the resuscitator bag, Edwina knew there was no way out of this.

Grace, I'm sorry, she thought clearly as the cubicle filled with people, the overhead and accessory lights glared whitely on; a babble of questions, orders, and controversy filled the room.

In a flurry of motion blood bags in pressure cuffs were pumped and hung, fluids opened, and big new IV lines inserted without benefit of sterile technique, the theory being that you could get better from an infection but not from being fresh out of hemoglobin and the fluids required to transport this important substance.

Someone was trying to get Grace's pressure with a stethoscope — it had now fallen too low to be picked up by the monitoring catheter.

126

After a time that seemed very long but was not, the ear-nose-and-throat surgery resident arrived with his endoscope and his electro-cautery kit.

"Hey," he said, assessing the scene without flinching as he made his way to the head of the bed, "short notice. Don't you folks ever make appointments?"

Edwina nodded in return; it was his way of calming people down. "What's the plan?"

He shoved a pillow under Grace's shoulders so that her head fell back, exposing the length of her throat.

"Go in below the blowout," he said, rummaging in his bag, "inflate the balloon on the tube — maybe compress the bleeding site, buy some time to get her to the OR." He frowned. "Depends where this sucker is. Aim me a light in here, will you? And gimme a blade — thanks."

In moments he'd cut through skin, fat, and muscle, laid bare the pale, glistening tracheal cartilage, and was slicing a window into it with the electrocautery blade, a tiny buzzing band saw of blue-white light.

A wisp of smoke and a whiff of burning flesh drifted up. The alarms on the monitors droned steadily. Plucking out the small square of tissue with a pair of forceps, he guided a long tube in through the opening he'd made and inflated the pilot balloon with a 10-cc syringe.

"Okay, squeeze."

Compressing the Ambu bag, Edwina watched a half pint of new blood bubble briskly up between the edges of the incision.

"Try it again," he said, and the bright, massive volume that followed made diagnostic comment unnecessary.

"Shit," he said. "Anybody have any other ideas?"

But no one did.

SEVEN

"My sympathies on the death of your friend," Martin McIntyre said, walking beside Edwina down York Street in the chilly dusk.

"Thank you." The streets were filled with homeward-bound commuters, rows of cars with headlights weakly gleaming. The air smelled of exhaust fumes, damp concrete, and approaching snow.

She had always meant to send Grace somewhere warm in winter. She had meant to take her to Litchfield, to meet and be fussed over by Harriet.

She had meant, she thought emptily, a lot of things.

"Will you make the funeral arrangements?" His long strides matched her own, his face thrust forward and shoulders hunched beneath his topcoat.

"No. Galilee Lutheran will probably be doing it. She was in the choir, and they take care of things when there's no one who can — " She bit her lip hard, tasting blood. "No one else," she finished. "Her sister's got her hands full already, I'm sure, and she's just a kid herself."

McIntyre nodded. "She'll get a good send-off from Galilee, though. I've been to a few of theirs. I go," he added, "to a lot of funerals."

She looked at him. "To see who's there, you mean? To pick up — " she paused at the silly word, "clues?"

He smiled. "No, just to pay my respects, like anyone."

Around them in an area of adult bookstores and XXX-rated movie houses, boys in tight pants and jackets too thin for the evening loitered on the stoops of crumbling brownstones, smoking cigarettes and waiting for who knew what.

A hooker wearing a black spandex halter and leather skirt leaned into the window of a squad car; the cop said something to her and she laughed, shivering as she tossed her mane of hair, which was orangey green beneath the streetlamp.

A skinny man in two-tone shoes cruised the street with his eyes, caught sight of the squad car, and turned away, nearly running into Edwina. "Hey, chicky," he whispered as he passed.

McIntyre hesitated. "Never mind," she told him, "people just like to talk. It's when they don't say anything that you have to worry," she added, wondering if Grace's

130

killer had spoken to her first.

They walked a while longer. "When you said you didn't get used to it," she began.

McIntyre glanced down enquiringly.

"I feel," she went on, "as if I could hurt someone. Only I don't know who to hurt."

"Yeah, well, I've got more bad news."

Her worry for Hallie Dietz flared afresh.

"No," he said, answering her look, "nothing new on the little girl. Her picture and description are out to the agencies and beat cops, Talbot's checking hotels and shelters, we don't think she got on a bus or a train, and there haven't been any juvenile . . ."

"Unidentifieds," she finished for him. "I guess that's the good news, then. What's the bad?"

He shrugged. "Just that if somebody's got a nine-year-old tucked away, they're doing a good job of hiding her. Time goes by, things get tougher, and it's been twenty-four hours now. Meanwhile Claymore's investigators, the ones he used to find her in the first place, they're blowing a lot of steam about client confidentiality."

"Can they do that? Isn't that obstruction or something?"

"Yes and no. We ask, they refuse. We subpoena, they'll appeal. We'll get them to talk to us if they want to keep their private licenses, but it'll take time. Meanwhile they'll shred paper and erase tapes, if there are any, minimize the damage if they can."

They were walking now between rows of small, bright shops, bookstores, clothiers, and restaurants. A door opened; music tinkled briefly and was cut off. The drifting aromas of coffee and food reminded Edwina that she hadn't eaten anything today.

"Damage?" she asked.

"Claymore's paying them," he replied, "through Hillerman, and it's not nice to give away the stuff your client is paying for if it has even the slightest chance of being used against him."

"Which if it didn't, you wouldn't be asking for it in the first place — to see if there's anything funny."

"Right, and they know that. Same goes double for lawyers, only they really can clam up and make it stick. Meanwhile we wouldn't need any of these jokers except for the worst part. When Talbot got over to probate-court library this morning, got the file on the custody proceedings, and opened it up, what do you think he found?"

"Nothing," she replied, guessing it from his voice.

"Right again. Depositions, hearing transcripts, social-work reports, medical testimony, investigators' statements — hell, things get lost, but I'll bet this stuff got lost on purpose."

"And the longer it takes to reconstruct, the hazier it all gets," she said. "Tracking down the people and getting them to repeat what they knew or found out — "

"Only not necessarily under oath this time," he put in. "Assuming we find them and they remember. And like I said, as time goes by . . ."

She looked at him, shocked, although she knew she shouldn't be. "You might have to put it aside?"

"Not entirely, and not tomorrow or the next day. But it's politics, Edwina. If a cop gets killed tonight, or some hotshot buying coke in the Hill section gets offed for his car and wallet tomorrow, or enough time goes by with nothing breaking — "

He lifted his hands, let them fall. "Hey, I don't pick my cases, I get them assigned to me. I'm not saying that's how this one will end up. But nothing good happens slow, Edwina. Not in this business, anyway."

They continued on in silence while she wondered how long it would take: an obituary, a funeral, maybe a memorial service at Grace's school.

No one to agitate for finding her killer,

though. Ghetto families were as short on clout as they were on groceries and jobs, and Grace's family was shorter on these than most.

So sooner or later the Dietzes and Claymores would go home, some new victim would occupy the front pages, and Grace would be forgotten along with the murdered lab tech, while Hallie Dietz became just another missing kid with her picture on the back of a milk carton.

Meanwhile the hospital didn't care if the end came with a bang or a whimper, as long as it came — and the sooner the better.

"Listen, do you have someone waiting for you? I mean," she hesitated, "I wouldn't want to interrupt your plans."

His eyebrows went up. "The little woman? Frilly apron and lemon-meringue pie, the good cop's long-suffering wife?"

"That's not quite what I had in mind."

They kept walking. "No," he replied after a while, "no one like that. You?"

"No. I thought I might buy you dinner."

His look showed he wasn't fooled. "Pump me for information is what you thought. I can see that brain of yours clicking away, so don't try to kid me. Hey, why should I tell you anything that's going to get you deeper in this than you already are?"

"Because," she replied, "I'm a nurse, and everyone knows nurses are harmless. It's why people will admit things to nurses they'd never tell a doctor — or a policeman, for that matter. We're extremely unthreatening."

McIntyre chuckled faintly. "That's true," he admitted. "Not that I think you're unthreatening, but I can see how some other people would. Less observant people."

He hesitated; taking advantage of it she looped her arm through his and moved him toward the nearest restaurant.

"About as unthreatening as a piranha," he added thoughtfully.

But after only the faintest further show of resistance he followed her in.

"So," she said when she had secured a back table, a pair of large, icy-cold martinis, and the attention of a waiter who stopped just short of genuflecting while delivering the drinks, as it was Edwina's habit to tip liberally and in advance. "Let's say I think I got the wrong baby in the hospital. I think I know who and where she is. What's my next step?"

"Next," he said, "you find yourself a heavy-duty law firm specializing in custody and child-welfare cases — like the one the Claymores got, Hillerman and Waugh."

He sipped his drink. "Assuming the lawyer thinks there's a basis for your claim — and

135

you've got money, no one takes a case like this on contingency — he writes a letter full of whereofs and therefores telling whoever's got the child that you're going to sue for custody. That's what Hillerman did."

"Why not just go straight to court?"

McIntyre shrugged. "Well, you've got to get things going somehow, find out the lay of the land. You write to them, they write back, and maybe they say something stupid, something that will help your case. So you give them that chance."

"Is that what the Dietzes did? Say something stupid?"

He ate the martini olive. "Nope. They may look a little thick, but they're not. They got a lawyer almost as big as Harold Hillerman, who as much as told Hillerman to take his case and blow it out his ear. Which," he sipped again, "was smart. Look a little weak or uncertain, a guy like Hillerman'll tear your throat out. Like a criminal case, winning by intimidation."

"Only Hillerman wasn't intimidated."

McIntyre chuckled. "A howitzer wouldn't intimidate that guy. Besides, Claymore's private guys got a load of evidence out of that clinic fiasco, stuff even the court in that one never heard, no one had dug it up back then. Hillerman knew he had a case, they couldn't dust him back," he finished. "But don't ask how I know that."

"Really," Edwina said. "Like what stuff?"

"Like whatever was in those missing files, for one thing." He looked disgusted. "Hey, it's easy. Dress up, go down there, act like you know what you're doing. Say you're somebody's paralegal, show halfway-decent ID. Take the file in a corner and bingo, fill it full of blank sheets. The real stuff goes in your pocket, and no one ever checks — not you, not the file folder. That's it."

"Wish I'd thought of it. Anyway, what happened after the Dietzes' lawyer wrote back to Hillerman?"

"The usual," McIntyre said. "Hillerman filed his affidavits in probate, petitioning for a change of custody based on kinship and the best interests of the child. And as you know if you were reading newspapers back then, the judge tossed it."

"I wasn't reading any newspapers." At the time, Tami and the *Bertram* — mostly Tami — had been uppermost in her mind; for a while, at least, he had seemed more interesting than any current event short of nuclear war, or even possibly including it. But like some briefly debilitating tropical fever, this period had passed without harm.

McIntyre shrugged. "Even when they did

get in front of a judge, it was all a lot of smoke blowing, not much substance. Here's this couple, no one knows who they are, come out of left field and say some other couple's kid is theirs." He made a noise of disgust. "Forget it — probate court said no probable cause, the Claymores' claims were speculative and self-serving, and in any case a change of custody wasn't in the child's best interest."

"But that wasn't the end of it."

"Not by a long shot. Could have been. Lots of times, what you get out of court depends on how sophisticated you are about going in. Hillerman's no fool. To him, the turndown was just routine. He appealed, and appeals out of probate go to superior court, a whole new ball game. You get to start over is what it comes down to."

"Fix your mistakes?"

"Yep. Because the main thing the lower-court judge said was that mix-up or no mix-up, he wasn't pulling any kid out of her home eight years after the fact — no matter what the fact turned out to be. His exact words, if I remember them, were 'In this courtroom, biology is not destiny.' And Hillerman took the hint."

"And went after something more for his second try."

McIntyre nodded grimly. "Hired back the

138

snoops and dug up all the dirt, scandal, and gossip he could find on the Dietzes. From the fees Claymore paid them, it must have been quite some operation — and no, I'm not going to tell you how I know that, either."

She didn't press. "And it worked."

"So it seems. Hearings were closed, the proceedings were sealed, but the superior court ordered family investigations, medical reports, and testimony, the whole nine yards. That led to the blood tests on the basis of what the investigations showed, and here we are."

Just then the waiter brought their orders. McIntyre looked pleased at the sight of sirloin, salad, and potato.

"Sir?" The waiter presented a bottle to him.

"Oh. Uh, no need. Just pour it, I'm sure it's fine."

The wine was a Cabernet with a velvety sheen and a bouquet of old oak, so dark it was almost black.

"In the joints I'm used to," he said with a laugh, "this comes in a jug. Have to drink it fast or it eats the enamel off your teeth."

"To Grace," she said, lifting her glass.

"To all of them." He matched her gesture and they drank in silence.

"You know," she said after a moment, "Grace reminded me so much of myself. I know, on the surface you'd think we couldn't be more different. I grew up a very privileged, sheltered girl with all sorts of expensive advantages — ”

“Money doesn't seem to have spoiled you,” he observed.

“Thank you. But it's more of a testimony to something or other that poverty didn't ruin Grace. By the time she was ten years old she'd seen things even grown-ups shouldn't have to see. And all it did was make her more of a born nurse than she already was — hard head, soft heart. And smart.”

Edwina sighed, remembering. “I'd have aimed her at medical school, but she said she didn't want to go. She said doctors didn't get close to the patients the way nurses could — didn't do for them the way she wanted to do.”

She stared at her glass of wine. “I watched her once, by the bed of a comatose patient. He was dying — I mean right in the act of dying, and he had no family or anybody there with him. She held his hand for half an hour while his heart rate dropped. When it was gone she kissed his forehead. Then she went off and sat by herself a while, but twenty minutes later she was back helping bundle him up for the morgue. She said she might just as well get used to the idea.”

“Was that how you felt when you first started nursing?”

She shook her head. "No. I was never a natural like Grace, I had to learn how to care. But she wanted it the way I did — to do something, to be someone who really mattered to people."

"Well," McIntyre said quietly, "I think you both succeeded. If," he added, "you don't mind my saying so."

She ducked her head in awkward acceptance of the compliment, surprised at herself for having talked so easily of her feelings. He had a way of listening, though, that made it seem quite normal to do so.

"One thing still bothers me," she said when the moment had passed. "If the Dietzes are lying, that gives them a motive to deep-six the blood tests. To hang onto Hallie."

"And to avoid prosecution," he reminded her, "if the DA finds a way around the statute of limitations — which he might. The Claymores say the switch was on purpose, remember, and that money changed hands."

"Fine, but what about the Claymores themselves? They pushed for the tests in the first place."

McIntyre chewed and swallowed. "Don't know. What I do know is their investigators handed in expense reports through last Friday. I assume they earned their money somehow."

"Really," she said, trying not to sound

eager. "And what do you imagine they were earning it on?"

He ate a sauteed mushroom. "Don't know that either. Claymore's last meet with them was Monday morning at seven-thirty in the Chelsea Memorial cafeteria, though. Which," he eyed her sternly, "you are not to repeat to anyone, because I don't want my little fly on the wall to get swatted, see?"

She nodded, speechless.

"Who knows," he went on skeptically, "maybe the guys just came in for coffee and a chat. Find out who Claymore likes for the Super Bowl, that sort of thing."

She found her voice. "You mean yesterday?"

"Yep. Which is why I'm looking just as hard at Claymore as I am at the rest of the bunch."

He smiled, not a pleasant smile. "Maybe that breakfast meeting was so Claymore's dirt digger-uppers could tell him they'd dug up something new. Something, maybe, that made him wish he'd never started all this in the first place."

"They're gone," Jennifer Stedman said tonelessly. "Both of them, and it's my fault. I wasn't paying attention."

It was just past eleven. Half an hour earlier, Edwina had gone upstairs alone to find her answering machine blinking at her; on the tape had been the message from Jennifer.

"Who's gone?" Edwina demanded now.

Jennifer looked up from where she slumped on the folding chair in the nurses' locker room just off Seven West.

"My old man and his wife, the ones I told you about. I was worried about Eric, we'd had another fight, and I just wasn't thinking."

She slammed a fist to her thigh. "Or not thinking hard enough, anyway. If I'd been — "

The locker room smelled of talcum, Jean Naté cologne, and the forbidden cigarettes people sneaked here. Taped to the wall was a square of mirror with a crack through it; above, a fluorescent light flickered meanly from behind a yellowed plastic screen.

Jennifer took a deep breath. "Anyway, I talked to the old people, explained again about the insurance, why he couldn't go home. And I offered them a compromise — for her to come here, instead — and they agreed. I'd even talked it over with my senior resident, and we all," she finished brokenly, "agreed it was the best thing."

"I see." Edwina seated herself on an old upholstered chair someone had dragged in, its fabric patched heavily with friction tape. "And then what happened?"

Jennifer rummaged in her lab coat pocket,

came up with fresh tissues, and blew hard. "Well, she got here about three. And it was fun, Edwina, they had a nice dinner, somebody sneaked them in a split of champagne — they enjoyed themselves. They laughed."

Her eyes filled with fresh tears. "Anyway, around eight the medication nurse found them asleep. Curled up in his bed like a couple of spoons with the TV on, she said."

"So she left them alone."

"Sure, only I'd changed his digitalis order this morning, so he was on four-hour vital signs. Which meant that at ten someone went in to take his blood pressure. Only," she finished, "he didn't have a blood pressure, and neither did she."

Jennifer's voice dropped. "She had a new prescription of sleepers, I wrote it for her last week at clinic. By the label on the bottle, she must have had it filled on her way here."

"Of what, Benadryl?"

"Nembutals." She glanced up defensively. "She'd been taking them for years. Sure, probably she was hooked on them, but heck — she was eighty years old, in constant pain, and couldn't sleep without them. And she wasn't abusing them. I mean, she was always lucid."

"And why make her life any harder?"

"Exactly. But I should have asked her when

she got here to let us put them in the lockbox. I just wasn't thinking."

"Oh, come on Jennifer, you weren't thinking about a suicide pact? Well, neither was I, kiddo, and neither are most people. No way you could have predicted this."

Jennifer bit her lip. "I'm not sure. Did I repress knowing she had them? When I didn't ask about them, did she assume I was inviting . . . maybe they thought I was just trying to get rid of both of them. And," she hesitated, "maybe I was."

She looked up. "Now I don't have to worry about them, do I? And they don't have to worry about each other. It's all wrapped up nice and neat," she finished bitterly, "because Dr. Stedman forgot."

Edwina sighed. "Jennifer. People are free. Just because you take care of them doesn't mean you get to make their choices. And even if you'd asked her about the pills, if she was that purposeful why wouldn't she have simply lied?"

"I suppose," Jennifer said, not sounding convinced. "If I hadn't been so preoccupied, though . . ."

"And if you weren't busy beating yourself over the head with it now. What's really wrong, anyway? What's Eric done that's got you so upset you're ready to blame yourself for everything?"

It was a guess, but Jennifer's face said it was on target.

"Not anything he did," she replied slowly. "I'm used to his jumpiness, not sleeping, losing his temper at the smallest little thing — hard to believe, but I'm actually used to all that."

She looked down at her lap. "But Edwina, he's getting so suspicious of me. It's like a nightmare. He says he thinks Tyler isn't his son. He wants to get blood tests so he'll have solid grounds for divorcing me."

"I see," Edwina breathed, feeling as if the scales had just fallen from her eyes. "Jennifer, are you all right? Because if you want me to stick around, to talk to anyone — with you or for you — I'll be happy to."

"No," said Jennifer, squaring her shoulders, pushing back the massy waves of her hair. "I mean, yes, I'm all right, and no, you don't have to talk to anyone. It's my job, I'll do it. Their kids are on the way in."

She got to her feet. "I needed someone to talk to myself is all. Someone who wouldn't repeat it or hold it against me later." She managed a smile.

Edwina got up, too. "Tyler's not with Eric, is he?"

"No, he's at my sister's. You know what I think? Eric's on something. Coke — there's a lot of it where he works." She managed a shaky laugh. "They're all so driven in the money business — even worse than me."

"Maybe," Edwina said. Or maybe, she thought as she watched Jennifer trudge back to the wards, he was just going crazy on his own. Plenty of people did.

Leaving the hospital, though, she found herself reflecting not upon Eric Stedman's problems but upon his accusation.

He's saying Tyler isn't really his son.

It was perhaps the dumbest remark Edwina had ever heard; nevertheless, it was also among the most enlightening. The theory it summoned to mind was simple, potentially destructive, and unprovable — except, of course, by tissue typing.

Only, to whom did the theory apply?

"Not," she said to Maxie, "until afterward." The black cat stepped into her duffel bag and crouched on the sweaters in it, glaring at her as if to say he didn't approve of this plan and would stop it if he could.

"Because," she said, heartlessly shooing him, "if I tell him what I'm going to try and he objects, which he will, and I do it anyway, which I'm going to — well, he's going to be furious, isn't he?"

She tossed a pair of blue jeans into the duffel. "Deep in his heart he thinks I need protecting, and besides, he's just a tiny bit jealous of his detecting turf. He's trying not to be, but he is."

Maxie stalked across the bedspread in order to communicate that he too was jealous of his turf, a chief element of which was his mistress, who kept leaving him alone in the apartment.

"He'll really be ticked off — "

Maxie's tail twitched; he was ticked off already.

" — but if I just leave — say, to get my mind clear, to get out of the hospital for a day or so, he'll be none the wiser."

Seeing the duffel, Maxie was plenty the wiser. And sadder.

"Anyone can understand a reason like that," she said, "so if I don't get anywhere on my own, I'll still be in the game. He'll still tell me what *he* finds out."

Maxie's yellow eyes expressed the opinion that if he ever told what he'd found out, his owner would be jailed for life on the basis of his shocking testimony.

Sighing, she rummaged in her closet. Buried at the rear of it she found two articles of clothing, one a white dress of the type described in nursing-uniform catalogues as "perky," V-necked with two large pockets in a gathered skirt, and the other a white matching slacks-

148

and-top combination whose vaguely military cut suggested no military authority whatsoever.

These she pulled from their hangers and tossed reluctantly at the duffel, along with a pair of white ripple-soled Nurse Mates shoes and two pairs of white support panty hose.

"Why," she asked Maxie rhetorically, "don't nurses just wear signs that say Kick Me?"

In answer, Maxie sniffed and slunk into a corner. She felt her resolve melting. He was after all a living creature, not some electrical appliance she could turn on and off at her convenience.

"Hey, guy," she whispered. "Want to go for a ride?"

Maxie's ears pricked, his eyes narrowing with interest.

"In the . . . *car?*"

He leapt back to the bed, circled the duffel with sudden enthusiasm, and streaked from the room, apparently feeling that if he was about to go on a trip he had better get started on his own packing.

Surely he would be better off here, she thought, even if it did mean another ration of kibble and water. But hours later when she looked for him again she found him curled in his carrying cage, asleep with the leather loop handle of his leash lying between his paws.

"Mrupp," he said grumpily, eyeing her.

She grabbed up the box of dry cat food and his water dish. "Oh, all right — you win, you pestiferous beast."

In addition to her duffel and a bag full of Maxie's supplies, the cage with Maxie in it made a nearly impossible burden; his full-throated yowls of triumph didn't improve matters. From the other apartments along the hall came the smells of coffee and bacon, the sound of showers hissing and electric shavers humming, radios tuned to the early morning drive-time programs.

A brand new day, she thought grimly, only not for Grace or Helene Motavalli. The idea propelled Edwina past the doors of people preparing to enjoy another chunk of life, not worrying about it being snatched from them.

"Morning, Miss Crusoe," the doorman said from his perch on a stool by the front door. "You on your way to stomp out some more o' them nasty diseases, there?"

It was Walter's standard greeting, no matter the hour or if she was entering or leaving. Only today it seemed entirely appropriate; yes, she thought, that's precisely what I'm on my way to do. She struggled from the elevator, whose gate had a nasty habit of opening when

150

she wanted it closed and closing when she wanted it open.

"Good morning, Walter," she said, kicking viciously at the recalcitrant gate; no sense letting it think it had got the better of her, even for a moment. "I don't suppose there's a hand truck around somewhere that I could borrow?"

Walter shook his head morosely. "Some'un else borried it an' never brung it back, that han' truck. I oughter go an' borry it home, son'time."

He frowned, possibly contemplating the proper timing of such a daring plan. "He'p you 'ith alla them?" he offered, making no move to get up.

"Thanks, I can manage." Taking help from Walter was always a mistake. It made him feel that one had become his ongoing responsibility, which in turn guaranteed several months of such smotheringly intense solicitousness — the meeting and screening of one's visitors, a stream of morbidly expressed commentary upon one's appearance and health, the examination of each separate item of one's mail under the guise of "sorting" it — that on the whole it was less taxing simply to accept no help at all. Certainly it was much less taxing for Walter, which was probably the whole idea.

Out in the parking lot she shoved Maxie's cage into the Fiat's right-hand seat and wedged her bags onto the floor; if they went in back she would have to sit so far forward her knees would lock beneath the steering wheel. Finally she sank into the driver's seat.

Which was where she belonged. Not loitering around the hospital playing research assistant, not wheedling progress reports out of McIntyre. Making progress herself.

Or trying, at any rate. It did cross her mind that before beginning a journey of this type, she ought to get that tire fixed. At the moment the flat lay useless in the trunk.

On the other hand, having a tire repaired was a good excuse to stand around a small-town gas station, shooting the breeze and inquiring after old friends. Now that she thought of it, in fact, she wished she had two flat tires: one for the town of New Carrolton where the Claymores lived and one for the Dietzes' home town of Albemarle.

Since, barring some sudden revelation in one, she intended to visit both.

EIGHT

For a nonphysician, there were three ways of examining medical records not pertaining to oneself.

The first was to go to work for an insurance company where such records were scanned, coded, sorted into diagnosis-related groups for statistical and benefit payment purposes, and stored in refrigerated rooms on platter-size computer tapes.

Edwina considered this method for approximately 1.2 milliseconds before putting it out of her head entirely and without regret.

The second method was to subpoena the desired information, a process requiring greater authority than she had and, more to the point, better credentials than she could fake.

This left the final method: going to wherever the original records were kept and reading them, a straightforward enough process assuming only that one set up one's opportunity with care, picked one's moment alertly, and felt nervy enough to risk getting caught.

Which Edwina did. Supporting her choice

of method was the fact that there were really only two kinds of nurses in the world: the kind who worked nights and the kind who didn't, the latter more numerous and vociferous by a factor of ten.

Thus any nurse who actually asked for night work was sure to be hired on the spot almost anywhere if she could show two things: a valid nursing license and a measurable blood pressure.

Which was how Edwina became a night staff nurse at the New Carrolton General Hospital in New Carrolton, Connecticut.

No one looked hard at her application or seemed to notice that the address she listed was the Butternut Inn, just off the old turnpike a few miles outside of town. Instead, the hospital's anxiously welcoming personnel officer checked her most recent employment reference by telephoning Julia Friedlander — this being another thing Edwina had counted on, having herself phoned Julia first — while Edwina waited in a small outer room whose yellow cinderblock walls, linoleum floor, and row of metal folding chairs made it resemble the intake area of a fairly enlightened minimum-security women's prison.

In a way it was just that. The nursing journals were full of New Carrolton's nakedly desperate ads for help. She very much doubted they could stand to wait around for a formal *vita* when such help unexpectedly presented itself, and she knew she was right when after a short wait she found herself invited back into the hospital's hiring office.

"Well, Miss Crusoe, we seem to be in order." The personnel officer at New Carrolton was a balding, eager fellow whose tenacious manner reminded Edwina of a leg-hold trap.

He peered at her, blinking as if he feared she might vanish. "But there is one more small thing," he hesitated. "You see, our eleven to seven shift is quite thinly staffed at present."

No wonder, for if New Carrolton's payroll department got any more tightfisted, the hospital would have to start paying its employees with little sacks of granola.

Meanwhile Edwina took the personnel officer's remark to mean that he was running the night shift on the boniest of skeleton crews, praying to God he could hire a few more nurses before the American Hospital Association pulled a surprise inspection — or worse, before some patient was injured and decided to sue for neglect.

". . . just a tad pressured to get somebody started," he exhaled hopefully.

"You'd like me to begin at once," Edwina said. "Of course I understand, and that fits my plans nicely, too. Perhaps someone could show me around right now? Then I'd be prepared to begin tonight, wouldn't I?"

He sagged in relief. "Oh! That would be . . . my goodness, why don't you just come along with me, Miss Crusoe."

Beaming, he fairly shot from behind his desk in his rush to finalize capture of her; if I were a meat animal, Edwina thought, I'd be hanging upside down by this time.

"Welcome," he said heartily, pumping her arm vigorously up and down, "and I hope you'll be happy here. We're a small place but friendly and extremely up-to-date for our size."

His hand was dripping wet, his eyes doggy with gratitude. For a moment she almost felt sorry for him.

Then her glance fell on the thick packet of pamphlets and forms assembled for new employees; on top of it lay a hastily typed letter of agreement listing her starting hourly wage.

One look and her guilt evaporated. Anyone hiring nurses on that sort of pay deserved deeply and truly to get stiffed.

"I believe I can report with confidence," the personnel officer burbled at her, "that New Carrolton offers what modern, forward-looking nurses want."

Right, if what they looked forward to was the poor farm. Somehow she doubted New Carrolton had one of those; not quite in line with the zoning ordinances.

"I'm sure it has what I want, too," she told him, matching his hearty tone.

And after tonight, she added silently, I'll have gotten it.

New Carrolton resembled a toy town trapped inside some small exquisite paperweight: rows of neat clapboard houses and venerable old maples, a halfdozen white steeples poking through the high bare branches.

Around the village green stood a perfect little post office, the general store and town hall, the Christian Science reading room, a tea shop ("Fresh scones"), a hardware store, and a dry-goods emporium. Each roof was topped with a frosting of perfect snow.

It all made Edwina wonder what would happen if you shook it, except of course that this was precisely what was not allowed in New Carrolton, a town so New England stiff-necked and old-money quaint that painting a house any color but white took a special zoning permit, and God forbid any billboards or fast-food joints near the village limits.

Still, the public library got new books: two of everything from the *Times* best-seller list,

Edwina noted with approval as she entered the red brick Carnegie structure. Also the *Boston Herald,* the *Wall Street Journal, Investor's Daily,* and the Value Line supplement.

The local paper was the *Clarion,* which although it lacked reports on the currency markets — New Carrolton's main cash crop being precisely that: cash — looked pretty good on town doings.

She flipped through a recent issue: births, graduations, marryings, buryings — all here, along with a list of recent real-estate transactions, the minutes of town meetings, and a feature called "The Chatterbox" that took up an entire page.

Gossip, apparently, was the *Clarion's* specialty: who had done what to or for whom, with whom, and in whose official presence. If you'd been local long enough you could read the why between the lines, and if you hadn't — well, if you hadn't then it wasn't any of your business anyway, was it?

It was indexed, she saw with pleased surprise, and on microfilm. Someone with a good idea of how money ought to be spent was getting some smalltown sociology down on plastic.

Carrying several labeled boxes of the *Clarion* reels, she seated herself before one of the library's three brand-new microfilm viewers and threaded the first strip into it. And there they were.

Jane Claymore in her engagement photograph, her smooth dark hair glossy as a bird's wing, her eyes bright. Next came a studio shot captioned Willet-Claymore Nuptials Held; she was Smith cum laude, he was Harvard out of Amherst, already a vice president in a big telecommunications conglomerate when he married.

Another couple of spins of the viewer and the social whirl began: benefit balls, auctions, and fund drives. Jane Claymore was merely a committee member at first but ascended swiftly as shown by shots of charity events on the Claymore grounds — the green expanses surrounding their pillared colonial mansion made the word *yard* ridiculous — festivities complete with striped tents, squads of frilly-aproned waitresses, and in one case a tuxedoed string quartet.

Then the procession of social triumphs was broken by a sad note: the obituary of William Claymore, Sr., industrialist and philanthropist, predeceased by his wife Amalie, survived by his son, William, Jr.; a daughter-in-law, Jane; and granddaughter Jill. After that, Jane Claymore's charity labors fell off sharply until the small, somber death notice for Jill Willet Claymore appeared.

And then there was nothing; as far as public doings were concerned it was as if the Claymores had fallen off the earth. No mention of the custody suit, certainly, such unpleasantness being a bit too much even for the *Clarion*.

Thoughtfully, Edwina rewound the last film strip and wrapped the fat rubber band securely around the reel. The final photos of Jane showed a thin, dissatisfied woman, her smile constricted to a grimace, eyes glittery as the diamonds in her earlobes.

Worry for a sick child affected some people that way, especially at the start. Later, parents softened; life simply couldn't be lived at a fever pitch of anguish.

But Jane hadn't softened; on the contrary, which made Edwina wonder what else had been going on in the Claymores' lovely home. Claymore himself was absent from many of the photographs in which he might have been expected to appear — the election-year gala that had brought out every other male Republican for miles, for instance, dinner at the Hunt Club likewise.

Thinking these things, she strolled from the library into the brilliant afternoon. Back in New Haven the snow would be dirty water by now, a gray winter sweat generated by the heat of commerce and forty thousand internal combustion engines, but in New Carrolton it

remained like some imperishable frozen con-
fection: white between the geometric side-
walks of the green, around the park benches,
and in the pointy shadow of the war-memorial
obelisk, pale blue in the deep shade at the
bases of the bandstand, whose new lattice
gleamed freshly on four of its eight sides and
whose rooster weathervane crowed from the
peaked roof.

Perfect, but having been brought up in just
this sort of groomed, moneyed perfection Edwina now felt chilled by it. Perhaps, she
thought, turning away from the undirtied
snow, there was some local ordinance against
its melting.

By the time she had eaten a sandwich at
the luncheonette on Main Street, bought a tin
of cat food for Maxie at Gristede's, and driven
back to the Butternut Inn, it was after four.

Her room was a frothy concoction of floral
chintz, priscilla curtains, braided rugs, and
antique furniture, all set against a wallpaper
patterned with huge, carnivorous-looking
cabbage roses. The private bath, in contrast,
was frankly modern and hygienic — a recent
addition, since for the modern guest old-
fashioned charm ended firmly where fa-
cilities-sharing began.

"Don't expect this all the time," she warned
the cat as she emptied the tiny can's contents

onto his dish. "Think of it as restaurant food."

While he ate she wound and set her alarm clock, hung a Do Not Disturb sign on the door, and lowered the window shades. Finally she opened the first-floor rear window about six inches.

"You're not going to make me sorry for this, are you?"

But Maxie was making no promises; barely glancing at her he slipped between sill and shade. The tip of his tail flicked once and he was gone.

Well, she told herself firmly, he would be back; he had after all a near-human understanding of the dangers of highways, and tiny cans of factory-minced offal sooner or later always proved more attractive than mice and mangled grasshoppers.

Turning her back determinedly on the window she undressed and got into bed, composing herself for sleep.

This proved less than difficult. She did so enjoy a room whose furnishings implied that one might reasonably, even happily, be journeying alone: one single narrow bed, a single nightstand and dresser, double towels for the wasteful or the frankly sybaritic. And she had been up the whole night before.

Mostly, though, she slept from determination: in just over seven hours she would begin her first night of work at New Carrolton General Hospital.

And for the kind of work she had in mind, she knew she had best be awake.

"Evan Connell is a fifty-four-year-old man who came in last evening with chest pains, productive cough, shortness of breath, and fever spiking to 39.5 degrees not relieved by aspirin."

Around the beige conference table the evening shift on New Carrolton's twenty-bed adult medical ward reported to the night shift.

"He's on aspirin, erythromycin, codeine, Cepacol lozenges p.r.n., Alupent nebulizers with postural drainage Q4 hours, vitals Q6, monitor his I and O's and push p.o. fluids."

"He's pretty mobile," the report nurse added. "You can tell them to send him downstairs for another chest X-ray in the A.M. You want to watch out, though; he likes his codeine so don't let him fool you. When he's really in pain, he stops coughing."

As Edwina had thought, she was the only RN on this floor for the night. Also at the table with her were two licensed practical nurses and one aide, the latter a very large, greasy-haired woman whose face resembled a pan of badly risen bread dough.

"Lydia Frick's back," the evening-shift

163

charge nurse said. "She stopped taking her digitalis and Lasix last week. Told her daughter she was sick of going to the toilet every half hour and if she ate another banana she'd turn into Chiquita."

Sympathetic laughter from around the table was quashed swiftly by the rest of the story.

"Unfortunately, she went into flash pulmonary edema this afternoon, down at the Diamond Mall, if you can imagine that. Paramedics got her tubed, but by that time she was pretty blue. On a volume ventilator now, 100 percent O_2 and wide-open drips, pupils fixed and dilated, not responding."

The charge nurse looked up. "Tomorrow Dr. Quinn's going to talk to her family and write a do not resuscitate order, but if you happen to find she hasn't got a pulse, don't run real fast to call a code, if you know what I mean."

Murmurs of agreement seconded this. Lydia Frick was eighty-five years old, essentially brain-dead, and equipped at the moment with a shred of heart muscle that, without the chemical kick her IVs were giving it, wouldn't have powered a frog's leg.

Swiftly, report on the fifteen other patients was given, the medication-cabinet keys were handed over, and in a flurry of coat gathering, time-sheet signing, and last-minute instruction giving, the evening shift departed.

At once the dough-faced aide pulled a blanket from the linen cart and lumbered toward the darkened patient lounge.

"You want me, call me," she said flatly.

Which left the two LPNs, whom Edwina was pleased to discover were smart, experienced, and extremely well organized, being as they were unused to having any help whatsoever. By 3:30 A.M. census was recorded, controlled drugs counted and signed off, the pharmacy report sheet filled out, vital signs gathered, meds given to the patients who required them, all the IVs mixed and labeled, and the remaining doses for the night set out on the top of the medication cart.

Back at the desk one of the LPNs pulled out a book and the other a crocheting project. Both had thermoses, sandwiches, and fruit, offered to share them, and looked relieved when Edwina refused politely.

Down the single corridor the rooms were dark, the silence broken only by the thrum of Lydia Frick's ventilator and the tweeping of her cardiac monitor.

It was a far cry from Chelsea Memorial where at this hour the desks would be crowded with interns and residents trying to write up thirty-six hours' worth of admissions notes, progress updates, and discharge summaries, meanwhile fielding calls for everything from tardy sleeping-pill orders to imminent cardiac arrest.

"Thanks," Edwina said, "I think I'll take a walk down to the vending machines, though. Either of you want anything?"

Neither did, so she headed for the main floor, which along with an automated canteen housed the medical records room.

Locked, of course, but this posed no problem. In addition to the narcotics-cabinet key Edwina possessed keys for the X-ray department, the kitchen, the cast room in the orthopedics clinic, the central supply storeroom, the chapel, and the morgue.

All hung on an enormous ring that was handed from shift to shift at the end of each report, this being cheaper than paying on-call staff personnel to come in and open these areas on the few occasions when night-shift workers needed access to them.

Meanwhile with only a vestigial emergency service — New Carrolton was a private hospital; ambulances went to the larger Winsted Trauma Center — the chances of a wee-hours admission were small.

Still, you had to be prepared, which was why Edwina's ring held also a key to the medical records room.

Sending up a prayer of thanksgiving — until

four hours ago she hadn't known how she would handle this part of the plan — Edwina glanced up and down the deserted hallway and then slipped into the room.

Inside, she stood still and took several deep breaths. No plan really prepared one for breaking and entering, even if the breaking happened to be more in spirit than in fact.

As she waited for her thudding heartbeat to slow, she thought it over once more.

Grace and Helene had been killed and Hallie Dietz taken by someone with a specific reason.

The simplest was to hide the fact that Hallie and Jill had been switched at birth, a motive for the Dietzes, or to hide that they hadn't been switched at all, a motive for the Claymores but one with a lot of holes in it.

At least, so far it had holes in it.

But there was another possibility, too, one that looked more likely the more Edwina thought about it.

It was clear that after long childless marriages both Jane Claymore and Maggie Dietz had borne daughters. What wasn't so clear was whether Bill Claymore and Oliver Dietz had each fathered one, or even that either of them could.

Thinking this, Edwina pulled a penlight from her pocket and made her way between tall shelves stuffed with file folders. Motives,

167

she was beginning to see, were a lot like diseases: sometimes the only way to diagnose one was to rule out all the others.

The shelves were open, alphabetically arranged and flagged with pale manila cards. Records of patients whose last names began with A went on for two and a half shelves, each about six feet tall and eight feet long.

B ran nearly to the rear of the room, where a glowing red exit sign over a service door lit up some wheeled wire baskets heaped with folders for refiling. Behind the baskets was a niche where the red glow didn't penetrate.

Dimly she glimpsed a desk, some straight chairs, and at the very rear of the area a long low table with something — most likely more unfiled folders — piled upon it.

She turned back to the metal shelves. The Claymores would have had their own private physician, most likely an infertility specialist if Edwina's theory proved accurate. But that sort of problem was studied at least in part through lab work, and in such a small town as this the lab tests were often done in hospitals.

Straining, she dislodged a half-dozen C files, toppling them down into her hands. Clatchett, Clattibey, Clavell . . .

Claymore, three files: one slender, one medium, and one very fat folder held shut with several rubber bands.

Wedging the others back into their places, she carried these to the desk area and drew out one of the chairs. As she did something shifted behind her; from the shadows came a long, miserable groan.

Edwina's fingers unclenched slowly. "Who's that?"

"Who's *that?*" a man's voice shot back.

Then he emerged: short, round, rumpled, and clutching a pint bottle of something in both his hands. From the cloud of fumes preceding him, she judged that he had already transferred most of the bottle's contents into himself.

He fumbled his glasses to his face. "Nurse. Might've known. Goddamned blight on creation, nurses. Can't a man have his grief in private anymore? What's that you got there?"

She looked down, saw she still clutched the file folders. "These? Oh, I'm just . . . well."

Hurriedly she searched for some reason he might believe, some excuse for needing the Claymore files. Unfortunately, she could think of no plausible reason for needing to read them with a penlight in a locked room in the middle of the night.

"Never mind. Don't care." Draining the bottle, he flung it at a wastebasket; the clatter made Edwina cringe.

"Lydia Frick," he said feelingly. "Most beautiful woman you ever saw in your goddamned life."

He sank into a chair. "I was twenty, she was forty — who cared? Most goddamn beautiful. Tomorrow I pull the plug."

"You're Dr. Quinn," she said with sudden comprehension.

He snorted. "Shitload of good it does me."

"I'm sorry. It must be very difficult for you, losing an old friend."

He squinted at her. "You ain't an old friend, though, are you? I know everyone in town, delivered half of 'em, yanked the tonsils out of the rest. Who the hell're you, middle the goddamned night?"

He struggled up toward the phone on the desk. "See about this. What're we paying the security guy, pick his nose?"

"Dr. Quinn," she said hurriedly, "please, I can explain. If you'd just let me — "

His gaze narrowed on the file folders.

"Claymore," he said disgustedly. "Might've known. More trouble'n they're worth."

Suddenly he didn't look drunk. Years of smalltown medical practice had taught him to focus his attention, hadn't it? And he was focusing it now, on her, with his hand on the telephone.

She gave in. "Do you want to hear all of

it? Or just the important parts?"

"I'll decide which are the important parts."

But to her surprise, when she finished he was snorting with laughter. "You think Billy Claymore's out shootin' up the citizens, protect his fair lady's honor?"

She frowned. "Or protecting something. What's so funny? I don't see anything a bit funny about any of this."

Quinn pulled off his glasses and scrubbed at his eyes. "No, but you're young, see — that's why. If poor Lydia could hear this, why, she'd laugh herself into a conniption fit."

He stopped. "Guess she's already had one of those, though, hasn't she? God, that woman had the most wonderful laugh on her. I remember we met up at somebody's funeral once, it doesn't matter whose, I made some comment to her. And she let out with a laugh — well, the whole room turned, you'd've thought she'd gone up and spit on the deceased. And she looks around at all the bereaved gone silent and kind of disapproving, you know, and she says clear as a bell: 'I hope when I'm gone all my friends have a drink and a good laugh on me, that's what I hope.' "

Quinn sighed. "That was what she hoped. So now I'm going to have to go try and do it, ain't I?"

He shook himself. "Anyway what's funny is you thinking Billy Claymore's sterile or impotent or anyway less than likely to prove it anywhere, anytime. Old Billy, he's what us old-timers used to call a swordsman. You old enough to know what that means?"

"It doesn't mean he's fathered any children."

"Nope," Quinn agreed, "but he has. I delivered two of 'em myself, put a stop to two more. Took his cash for all of those right there in my hand."

He snorted again. "Kinda suggests to me he helped make them babies, 'less you believe he's a softhearted fella, help get ladies out of trouble he never helped get 'em into. And if you believe that," he added, "you're even younger than you look."

"No," she said. "I suppose not. But what about her?"

Quinn looked wise. "Uh-huh, I see what you're after. Think maybe poor Janie picked herself up some consolation and got herself in trouble on it? Hell, I doubt that. She's got about as much use for men as I got for a rubber crutch."

He reached out and took the files. "Nope. Girlie, you're barking up the wrong elm on this one. All Janie ever wanted was a Claymore baby and the only reason she wanted it was old man Claymore. And a Claymore baby is what she got," he added, "I'll bet. Although whether or not she hung onto it, that's another matter. That one was outside my jurisdiction, you might say."

"Old man Claymore? What's he got to do with it?"

"His money," Quinn said flatly, "that's what. Left it all in trust for Billy's kid. Lots of ways you can play a trust fund like that, you know how."

He dropped the files into one of the wire baskets. "And I happen to know they got a place in Switzerland they could do it from, too, the Claymores. Old country doctor like me, I hear all the dirt."

He turned. "But look, before you go gettin' all excited, thinkin' they've maybe got hold of this other little girl and they figure on collecting somehow — well, I'll let you in on something else. Billy *could* swing a thing like that, sure. Hell, he's got connections so deep in the muck he needs hip boots to find 'em all. Only," he finished, "deep in his heart he's too chicken for what you're talking about, an' so's she."

"I'm not sure — "

"I mean," Quinn said, "killing somebody and kidnapping somebody else to clear the way for your finagling. That's what you're talking about, right? That maybe there really was a switch, and this girl is Jane Claymore's daughter — only she isn't Billy's. That'd put the kibosh on the inheritance, all right. But if that's so, Janie would know it, wouldn't she? And to prove the child was hers would let that other cat out of the bag — so why start it all up in the first place?"

Edwina had pondered this point at length herself. "Sure, but she might not have understood that, at the beginning. Or maybe she thought she could get around it somehow, didn't know until too late that she couldn't. Or — "

She looked up as a new idea struck her. "Look, what if it doesn't put the kibosh on it? What if all she needs is to show that her daughter is a child born to her during the marriage to get the trust fund to pay? What if the trustees don't even want to know the gory details of the — "

Quinn's chuckle interrupted her. "First of all, even if the trustees don't want to know, whoever's next in line for the money's going to fight like the dickens. And if they don't — well, what's your play-by-play? How's the murder part supposed to happen?"

He held up two fingers. "Either he finds out the truth and starts killing folks to hide this deep, dark family secret, or at the last minute she has a change of heart, panics at the thought of him finding out, maybe divorcing her over it, and starts blasting away at folks herself."

"Right. Exactly. Either one of those. Why not?"

He shook his head. "You still don't understand, do you? Billy's about as in love with his family honor as I am with this desk, here, and Janie isn't going to have any change of heart 'cause she hasn't got a heart to have a change of."

In the glow of the exit sign, Quinn's bald scalp gleamed pinkly. "Besides, like I said, it strikes me murder must be a lot like surgery. Takes more than a reason and the know-how. It takes nerve." He got up and moved toward the door.

"Claymores," he snorted, "hell. Before they could shoot somebody you'd have to give 'em spine transplants, 'cause for all their money neither one's got the backbone of a pollywog."

By ten the next morning she was on the road, having told the regretful but unsurprised New Carrolton recruiter that she wouldn't be staying after all.

Beside her Maxie slept the sleep of the satisfied adventurer now that the mud and gravel had been dug from between his toes, the stickleburrs combed out of his fur, and a gash above his eye cleaned out and anointed with bacitracin.

Edwina, in contrast, was entirely unsatisfied. There was no laboratory test to diagnose guilt, and people didn't always behave in character or even in their own best interests. So despite Dr. Quinn's opinion she had phoned Martin McIntyre and left a detailed message for him — a message, she felt sure, that was going to get her into trouble.

Still, McIntyre would know how to find out if any Claymore agent tried tapping the trust fund. Such things could be fiddled, she thought, especially if enough money was involved. If they'd made a preemptive strike, one or perhaps both of the Claymores might win big, depending on how the fund was set up and managed.

And as Quinn had pointed out, even if they did show up later with the child it wouldn't prove they'd committed murder; they might still wind up with all the marbles.

Meanwhile, there was Albemarle still to be visited. At the prospect Edwina's foot pressed the accelerator; the Fiat responded with a growl and a thrilled burst of speed.

Oh sure, she thought sourly; fine for you. All you have to do is burn gas and not get another flat.

176

Albemarle was not a prosperous town like New Carrolton but a hard-bitten burg in the Housatonic Valley, built on factory money and crumbling now that the factories had pulled out — or, in a few notorious instances, had been burnt for their insurance policies.

There would be no microfilm, no new best-sellers or Value Line supplements in the Albemarle public library. There would be no bandstand, no charming village green.

Instead there would be ramshackle little taverns, their brick-patterned asphalt siding peeling off in strips. There would be rusted jalopies teetering on blocks, leaking oil onto the weed-choked driveways.

There would be tight mouths, slammed doors, and narrowed, suspicious eyes. And there would be Holly Ribolow.

Speeding down Route 8 toward the smoke-less smokestacks and the abandoned ware-houses, Edwina realized afresh how much she didn't want to see her old Chelsea colleague, how firmly she had left Holly Ribolow out of her calculations.

Her conscious calculation at least. As if Holly could be left out; Holly, who had never let anyone leave her out of anything.

Edwina didn't want to know what trouble and the years might have done, preferring to remember Holly as she had been: feckless, rebellious, and utterly unsuited to nursing, but with a grin that was wholly irresistible.

Easing the Fiat across the lanes, she followed the big green marker sign: Albemarle, Keep Right. Even while checking the map before coming here, she had continued pushing Holly to the back of her mind.

It was no doubt where Holly would wish to remain.

Too bad she couldn't.

NINE

The Albemarle Clinic was a red brick building squeezed in between a defunct muffler shop and a factory outlet store that specialized in frayed towels, miscut blouses, and plastic shoes.

As Edwina drove slowly by, several large blue-jeaned women with lank hair and bad complexions were herding rambunctious children in and out of this store, whose sign — red poster paint slopped onto butcher paper — advertised Sale On Kids' Winter Togs!

Togs, Edwina thought dismally. The day any of those kids wore anything resembling togs — any garment that didn't appear when brand-new to have been fished out of a Salvation Army box — would be a miracle. And miracles, by the look of it, were just one of the many things Albemarle was fresh out of.

The phone booth on the corner held no phone book, only the slashed empty shell where one should have been, so she dialed information.

Holly's number was unlisted, which meant

she still lived here in her old home town. Not much wanting to be found by anyone who had to look her up, though. Or visited at work, either, if she was still employed at the clinic.

But probably she was; when it came to troubles hiring help, New Carrolton didn't have a patch on this place, which was now a walk-in facility for the poorest of Albemarle's poor. Meanwhile with her nursing license lifted and her own reputation still to bear, Holly would have been lucky to get hired mopping up after autopsies anywhere else.

Sadly Edwina mounted the cracked concrete steps and crossed past a row of beat-up molded plastic chairs. On the admitting desk, an old black-and-white TV was snowily showing an episode of "The Young and the Restless." Slumped in the chairs, half a dozen patients stared at the screen.

Edwina approached the desk. Over it hung a cardboard placard inexpertly lettered in thick black strokes of magic marker:

PRESENT PUBLIC ASSISTANCE DOCUMENTS
WHEN REGISTERING

"Name?" inquired the nurse sitting guardlike behind the chest-high barrier. She was perhaps twenty-five with faintly bulging blue eyes and skin the color and texture of an old gravel road. Pinned to a uniform that long ago had been white, her name-tag said Tiffanye Pritchett, RN.

"My name is Edwina Crusoe, but I'm not here to see a physician. I'd just like to — "

Tiffanye dragged her bored gaze from the television to a box of file cards and pulled one out. "Address."

Edwina looked at Tiffanye. "100 York Street, New Haven," she replied evenly.

"How do you plan to pay for this visit?"

From Tiffanye's earlobe a greenish loop of metal dangled. Distantly Edwina wondered what would happen if she reached across the desk and yanked hard on the earring.

Tiffanye fastened her unpleasant stare on Edwina's face. "I said," she repeated distinctly, "how do you plan to — "

"That's what I thought you said. Don't you even ask people what's wrong first? What kind of symptoms they're having, if it seems to be an emergency or not?"

"We don't take emergencies." Tiffanye's face went flat. Apparently a refusal to be bullied was a new experience for her and one she did not much enjoy.

"Emergencies," she recited, "they have to call a ambulance on the pay phone outside because we don't take — "

"Right," Edwina said. "You don't take emergencies."

Then she inhaled deeply several times. If she didn't calm herself right now there would be an emergency here, and when it was over Tiffanye would be in no shape to use any telephone, public or private, ever again.

"I would like to speak with Holly Ribolow, if she's here."

"Personal visits not allowed," Tiffanye shot back.

"Of course. I understand." So Holly did work here. "I'll wait, then, or come back later when it's convenient for her."

"No waiting unless you're with a patient."

Edwina smiled carefully at Tiffanye, who was clearly wielding the few small powers she had just for the meager enjoyment of it.

Someone tapped her shoulder.

"You," she told Tiffanye, "are the rudest, nastiest, saddest, and most thoroughly unpleasant excuse for a nurse I have ever — "

"*Edwina.*"

"What?" She swung around.

Holly Ribolow was a small red-haired woman with hurt-looking brown eyes, a stubborn chin, and a generous sprinkling of freckles on her sharp-angled face. She wore a navy blue uniform pantsuit whose permanent press had been battered out by too many washings, white uniform shoes no amount of polish could ever renew, and a most unwelcoming expression.

Once, in nursing school and after, she had been Edwina's friend. But that was before Holly had been asked to leave Chelsea Memorial's employment, at a time when Edwina herself was so junior that she could do nothing about Holly's dismissal.

Later, when Holly got herself in real trouble and the scandal over the Albemarle Clinic blew up, Edwina had tried to help her. But no amount of string pulling could help a nurse who assisted in the clinic's baby-selling activities as Holly had.

At least no amount done by Edwina could, especially while public opinion was still so outraged, although Holly had refused to believe this and had ordered Edwina permanently out of her life. That was why Edwina had left a visit to Albemarle for last, hoping she wouldn't have to make one and not even wanting to think about it in advance. Holly didn't want her, and facing Holly's rejection again made the old pain of losing her friendship seem new and fresh.

"What are you doing here?" Holly demanded now.

Edwina opened her mouth to answer, remembered Tiffanye who was listening with greedy interest, and thought better of it.

"Never mind," Holly sighed, "come on. Unless," she added, "you want to get me fired out of this dump again."

I, Edwina thought, didn't get you fired the first time. But this too was probably a sentiment better left unexpressed, so she followed Holly from the clinic to the chill gray street.

"Oliver Dietz, he always was a cheap little bastard," Holly Ribolow said. "Money is evil, poverty is pure, all that crap. As if he was ever short of a buck," she finished bitterly.

Slopping hot water from a kettle into two mugs, she spooned lumps of instant coffee into them. "Creamer in this?"

Edwina glimpsed the jar of white powder. "Black is fine."

On the wooden table in Holly's drab kitchen stood a pair of plastic salt and pepper shakers, a jug of ketchup, and a saucer containing a lump of margarine that resembled lard. A yellowed philodendron struggled in a pot made from half a milk carton.

Holly smacked the cups down. "But I haven't seen him since high school. Anyway, why should I help you get their old medical records?"

"For old times' sake?" Edwina suggested, not meaning to be taken seriously. She sipped politely at the bitter brew, then set her cup on the paper napkin.

Holly frowned. "I guess you're not used to the store brand, you always did go first class."

"And you always envied me for it," Edwina said, more sharply than she had intended.

The house was a stucco box in a crumbling neighborhood of other stucco boxes. As she sat there Edwina could hear the furnace roaring and feel the draft from the ill-fitting windows.

"You know," she told Holly, "there was nothing I could do about your license. After the clinic thing, I mean — all the board wanted was your personnel file. They never asked me to talk about what you were like at Chelsea, and I never did."

Which from Holly's point of view was fortunate, as what Edwina would have said wouldn't have been very helpful to her. On the contrary: lateness, or not showing up at all; doing what she shouldn't do, not doing what she should until she'd had to be let go — all the while, of course, protesting the unfairness of her dismissal.

Holly's shoulders moved resentfully. "Doesn't matter. I didn't lose the license over Chelsea anyway. I lost it over the clinic — although I still say none of it was my fault. I just kept quiet and he helped me out was all. You'd think I was an ax murderer the way the papers made it out."

By "him" she meant her old boss, the clinic director; by "help" she meant keeping quiet about a guy who stole people's babies and sold them. The thought must have showed on Edwina's face; Holly's lips tightened.

"When he offered me money the first time, Randy — my little boy — was sick. He needed ear surgery, he was crying all the time because it hurt, and I didn't have medical on him. What was I going to do? I was losing my apartment that month, too — if I hadn't shut up, I'd have been out of work besides."

She jerked her head defiantly. "So you just tell me you'd rather your son went deaf and was put on the street," she demanded. "You just look me in the eye and tell me that."

Edwina sipped from a cup that smelled of dish detergent and said nothing. At the front of the house a door slammed; a boy's deepening voice called out.

"Ma? I'm home." Heavy footsteps went down a hall, then thumped outside. In the narrow yard beyond the kitchen window a gangly kid of about seventeen appeared, his hair red like Holly's. With a careless toss he put a basketball through the hoop mounted on the garage, caught it, and sank it easily.

"And what about now?" Edwina asked. "How are you managing? I don't suppose the clinic pays much."

Holly shrugged. "We get along. Only . . . he wants to go to college, Randy does. But he's not tall enough for a basketball scholarship, the academic ones are like hen's teeth, and we're not quite poor enough for the loans, if you can believe that."

She stared stonily at her hands. "I haven't told him yet, but he isn't going. Not next year, anyway."

Which meant never; once you were out of the loop, the loop spun on without you. Edwina glanced around. "Second mortgage?" she suggested cautiously.

Holly's answering laugh was a sharp, sad bark. "You think I own this place? Even if I did I couldn't make the interest on a second mortgage."

She put her cup down. "Look, you'd better leave. You're just going to get me in — "

"I can get Randy a scholarship." The words were out of her mouth before she knew she would say them.

Holly stared. "You can't either do that. Don't you lie to me, Edwina."

"But I can. My father went to Fitzwilliam and he left them a scholarship fund." Edwina shrugged. Harriet could put the fix in easily.

187

"Hey, your kid might as well get it — if you help me."

Holly bit her lip. "What if what you're looking for isn't there? Maybe they go to a doctor in New Haven now."

"But she had the baby there, so they went before that, didn't they? And that's what I want to know about," Edwina pressed. "Before."

We tried for years to have her, Dietz had said.

Which meant one of them might have had fertility problems, might have tried to find out what those problems were — and whose.

The evidence would be at the clinic: if Oliver Dietz couldn't be a father, then he wasn't. And just as with William Claymore, if that was true it was worth learning — and if not, worth ruling out.

"Just try," Edwina told Holly. "If you can't get the files, or if there's nothing there, I'll still help you. But only for the truth," she added. "If you lie, or leave something out . . ."

The threat was itself a lie; there was no guarantee she would be able to check anything. More likely the opposite — that when McIntyre caught up as he must already be trying to do, he would tell her to quit and she would have to. As Holly had learned, there was only so much trouble a nurse could get into and

188

still hang onto her nursing license.

Outside the window Holly's kid kept on trying for baskets, missing but not quitting, shrugging when the ball fell outside the rim. As Edwina watched he faked out an imaginary guard, ducking under and lobbing again: two points.

He was good for high school, but college hoops would eat him alive and he looked smart enough to know that.

Smart enough, too, not to let it spoil the game for him. His boyish face was smooth, intent on the simple pleasure of shooting a basketball alone on a winter afternoon.

She wondered what he would say when he found out he was going to be a Fitzwilliam man.

Maxie paced, making obstreperous noises as if to say that he liked midnight runs much better than days spent trapped inside a too-small wire cage and what was she going to do about it?

"Hey, buddy, you were the one who had to come along."

But there was time for one more ramble while she satisfied the last of her own curiosity, so instead of heading straight for the interstate and home she dug out the tattered road map.

The Dietzes' address was on a blacktop lane

curving between orchards, pastures, and the occasional house lot that had been carved out when some farmer got strapped at property-tax time. The split-level ranches on the raw new plots looked embarrassed, as if they knew they were there on account of someone's trouble and weren't really welcome at all. Then came a stretch of water-company land, barbed wire and white pine crowded close to the road, the deep woods shadowy and silent.

Through the half-open car window came smells of evergreen and ferns, the trickle of water and rush of wind high in the big old pines. Maxie stood on hind legs, gazing hungrily out.

"Not yet," she told him, wondering if she had missed the mailbox. Then it appeared, past the last vine-snared fencepost with its rusting yellow No Trespassing sign. Through a narrow gap between dense cedar hedges, an unpaved way led in.

She reconsidered after twenty yards of washboard ruts, but too late; bracing herself she swerved and swore, shot a glance at the rearview mirror, and hoped she wouldn't see a Fiat muffler back there.

On either side leafless brush closed in; only after several long wincingly harsh scraping sounds did it fall away, thinning to reveal a clearing with a yard, a house, and outbuildings

— but not the yard, house, and outbuildings she had been expecting.

The dwelling was octagonal, low-roofed, walled on four sides with plate glass sheets divided by weathered cedar timbers. An irregularly shaped deck on several levels resembled a Chinese garden, its stone urns, clay pots, and wooden tubs harboring an elaborate and flourishing bonsai collection.

To one side a terrace spread, paved with flat red slates and sheltered by an arbor that led to a greenhouse, a weathered cedar shed, and a larger, many-windowed building that might be a studio. Behind stood whitewashed chicken coops, a mulched garden plot, and a rail-fenced area beside what was apparently the sheep barn.

Blinking, Edwina tried to reconcile this place with her memory of the Dietzes. This didn't look like the home of a pair of aging hippies living out some adolescent back-to-the-land fantasy. It looked, more credibly, like heaven on earth.

She got out to check for dogs, but there weren't any. No pet pigs, either; apparently that story had been more legend than fact.

Apparently also the Dietz sheep weren't the kind that had to be herded about; from the look of the place, they probably came when their names were called and stood obediently at shearing time.

"OK," she opened the latch of Maxie's cage, "come on. But don't run off. I don't think I could find you here in the dark."

Maxie swiveled his velvet-black head to gaze up at her. Not for the first time she wondered what lay behind his eyes, so thoughtful and utterly alien. At the sound of her voice, instead of streaking immediately for parts unknown, he fell into step with her, padding sedately and pretending for the moment to be civilized.

No grass to mow, she saw: creeping myrtle and some kind of low evergreen shrubbery instead. No paint to freshen; cedar weathered a lovelier gray. No upkeep at all but the occasional cutting back of the wisteria twining on the terrace arbor. Which was how they'd done it, just the two of them.

Or part of it, anyway, for surely it took help keeping such a place in shape, even without any yardwork or painting: the garden, household chores, animals, a mail-order wool business, and of course the raising of a child.

As she gazed about the blue shadows lengthened; the breeze took on an edge of ice. Every view was composed as carefully as a painting, each small detail purposeful.

The doorbell was a real bell, its cast-iron clapper equipped with a knotted leather thong. The kitchen garden, a brick-edged black loam oblong protected by a propped-up cold frame, was a botany book of herbs: rosemary, chives, oregano, chervil, thyme, mint geranium — a thing of beauty and a joy forever.

Only maybe not forever. Stepping up onto the deck, Edwina began to have a bad feeling. From here she could see straight into the many-windowed studio, the slanting sun illuminating the objects ranged within: jewel-like colors and unearthly shapes, some of strands thin as spider silk, others made from yarn as thick as babies' fingers. The simplest piece was a tapestry on a stainless-steel rod: azure, purple, and aquamarine on a silvery background. Hanging in stillness, the fabric seemed to ripple slowly like deep water.

The strangest was difficult to look at and yet seductive: a shell shape, coiling inward. Squinted at hard, the piece was flat, but when the effort to see it as flat was given up it sprang at once back to its illusory three dimensions.

The studio was kept with military neatness: wool skeins on pegs, enormous cones of thread, tapestry frames lined according to sizes from foot-square to man-tall. Under one skylight stood a cherry floor loom, a tall warping reel like a balsa carousel beside it.

On the walls, dozens of posters framed in

strips of brushed aluminum announced dates of gallery shows of new work by Margaret Dietz. Most were in New York, a few in Boston, and one — the largest and apparently most important — had been in Los Angeles.

All were at least ten years old. Puzzled, Edwina squinted at the collection, which ended oddly and suddenly. Maggie Dietz's art was remarkable enough but the dates on these posters were more curious, for unless she kept newer posters elsewhere or no longer saved them, this amazingly talented textile artist seemed not to have had a show in over a decade.

Ten years and two months, to be precise.

Beside her on the deck step, Maxie stopped washing his face and got up, ears pricked and tail stiffened into a question mark. Moments later a brown-skinned woman in corduroy pants and a gray wool cardigan came around the corner of the house, stopping short when she saw Edwina.

"I'm very sorry," Edwina said, "I didn't know anyone was — "

"Who's there, Mom?" The little girl was groomed and dressed with care: hair neatly cornrowed and braided with turquoise-bead tassel-ends, tiny silver earrings, and a hint of pink lip gloss. She wore a pink warm-up jacket, jeans, and high-top sneakers with pink ballet ankle warmers bulked over them.

"Oh, a kitty," she crooned, crouching. "Here, kitty." In response Maxie sat firmly down.

Good boy, Edwina thought, as all at once she didn't want to provoke this woman. The sweater she wore had deep roomy pockets; somehow her hands had gotten into those pockets without her ever seeming to put them there. To keep them warm, maybe.

As Edwina wondered, the child sprang out. "Mom, I just want to go see the — "

"Get inside." The order came sharp as a pistol shot.

With a last yearning glance the child shrank back, vanishing behind the house to wherever she had come from.

"You are on private property." The woman stepped nearer.

"Right," Edwina said. "Come on," she told Maxie.

Later she thought perhaps that her shoe had caught or that Maxie had somehow gotten between her feet. Surely there was no sense of being pushed, though the woman was near enough to do so.

At the moment all she knew was that she'd lost it somehow, arms pinwheeling uselessly as she toppled from the stairs. An instant later the brick-edged path socked the breath out of her.

Fifteen feet up, the woman gazed impassively at her. "You all right?"

She wiggled her toes; spinal cord intact. Cautiously turned her head. When sensation didn't vanish abruptly, she felt emboldened to sit up.

Bad move. "Ugh," she said as a fistful of pain jammed its way determinedly under her breastbone.

Nasty, but not sharp, and she wasn't short of air. Bruise, then, or at worst a cracked rib. People had fallen down steps before and survived.

Damn, that hurt. "Prut?" Maxie inquired, sniffing anxiously.

The woman appeared at the foot of the steps. "You'd better come inside."

Bunches of dried herbs hung from the huge exposed beams in the Dietzes' big old-fashioned kitchen. At least at first glance it looked old: rag rugs on the plank floor, a potbellied stove, a claw-footed porcelain sink. Ajaxed to snowy whiteness. From a hook by the door hung a galvanized washtub; below it squatted a wooden object shaped like an overturned pail with a broom handle sticking from its top: a butter churn, Edwina thought. The room seemed to shimmer with cleanliness and smelled sweetly of yeast softening in warm milk.

At the bleached pine counter the woman was pouring something hot into a cup, tasting it, then filling another.

Edwina sat in the cricket chair by the stove, which gave off faint crinkling sounds like aluminum foil being crumpled. At her feet Maxie stretched in the warmth, relaxed but watchful.

"This is very kind of you," she said, accepting the pottery mug the woman offered. Mulled wine, she realized, its sharp spicy fragrance rising in a steamy cloud. The woman's name, she felt sure, was Hepzibah Scott.

A pretty name, Maggie Dietz had said.

"Here," the woman said, holding out two white tablets. "You might feel better later if you go ahead and take these now."

Aspirin; Edwina examined them carefully before swallowing them gratefully. "I can't believe I was so clumsy. Really, I'm sorry to put you to all this — "

"No trouble." The woman moved easily about the kitchen, as if it were her own. On the counter stood canisters of flour and sugar, glass jars of peas, beans, and rice. From an open shelf she took down a brown mixing bowl and began measuring flour into it.

"So," she said, "you found your way here all right."

Edwina looked up in surprise, the drink already spreading a soothing glow through her chest.

"Mrs. Dietz said you might come," Hepzibah went on, pouring a smaller bowl of liquid into the larger bowl. "She said you were like a rat terrier she had once. Real smart, but once it had hold of something it wouldn't ever let go."

She picked up a wooden spoon. "And here you are."

On balance, Edwina thought Maggie Dietz's comment might as well be taken as a compliment. "Did she say why I might come?"

"Oh, yes." Hepzibah began stirring the heavy mixture in the bowl. "She said you were the kind who would want to see things for yourself. Ask a lot of questions, probably, about a lot of things that aren't any of your business."

Fair enough. As her eyes adjusted to the room, Edwina saw the dishwasher concealed behind a pair of shirred gingham panels, freezer and refrigerator doors veneered in pine. The black iron stove gave heat, but cooking was done on a gas range that looked about as old-fashioned as a fighter jet. From a varnished block bristled a brace of knives worthy of a French cooking school.

"You could have stayed inside until I went away. I'd never have known you were here."

Hepzibah stopped her stirring, pushed up her sweater sleeves, and resumed work, the muscles in her forearms moving strongly as she prodded the stiffening dough. "Why would I do that?"

"Mrs. Dietz might have asked you to," Edwina suggested.

Hepzibah's smile was amused, her teeth white as a toothpaste ad. Dentures, but technically beautiful and well kept. The woman's face was lean and delicately boned, with dark eyes, full lips and a long, straight nose whose thin flaring nostrils made her look Egyptian.

"I stopped," she said, "doing everything people asked me to do a long time ago. Do you want another cup of that?"

Edwina sat forward, winced. "No, thank you. I have to be — "

Hepzibah took the mug briskly, refilled it, and handed it back. "This is the last of it. I'll make sure you're fit to drive before I let you go."

The stove and the wine were already doing their work. But the longer she stayed, the more Hepzibah Scott might say. As if understanding this, Maxie curled up with one paw over his eyes.

Hepzibah understood, too. "What they're telling everybody, the Claymores — it's garbage."

She pronounced the name as if it tasted bad, scattered flour contemptuously on the counter and dumped the ball of dough onto it. "I was there. I saw Hallie the day she was born, and I've seen her every day since. I know that child like my own."

"You came to work here then? Right from the hospital?"

"Came to *live* here," Hepzibah corrected, pummeling the ball of dough with floured hands. "They needed help, I needed a place to get away from . . . where I had been. One hand washed the other."

Her face closed briefly on some memory.

"They were a pair of children themselves," she said, "but they grew. Babies, you let them, they'll grow *you* up pretty fast."

A small shy face peeked from the darkened doorway of a staircase. Big brown eyes moved from Edwina to Maxie's sleeping form, then hesitantly fixed on Hepzibah.

"Mama? I'm hungry. Are we going to have . . ."

"Come here, girl." Hepzibah's voice was mild, but there was no mistaking the authority in it. Youngsters in this house did as they were told, plain and simple, or suffered the swift, sure consequences.

And were the better for it, perhaps. Confidently, the child stepped into the room and approached Edwina, offering her hand with a poise that belied her age.

"Hello. My name is Rebecca Scott. What's yours?"

The child's fingers were soft and cool. "My name is Edwina Crusoe, and this is Maxie."

Behind Rebecca, Hepzibah Scott's face smoothed into a look of pride. "Is your homework all finished?"

"Yes, ma'am, all finished. Pleased to meet you," the child said to Edwina. For a moment it looked as if she might curtsy. Then her gaze returned longingly to Maxie. "Does he bite?"

"No. Or scratch, either. You can play with him — if it's all right with your mother," Edwina added. At the word "play," Maxie got up and twitched his tail hopefully.

"Upstairs," Hepzibah said. "Take an apple. I'm starting supper as soon as I get this bread dough rising."

Rebecca opened her mouth to say something, then thought the better of it. Plucking an apple from the bowl on the oak sideboard, she made kissing sounds at the cat, then turned back to the sideboard for an instant; moments later the two of them had vanished up the stairs.

"She's beautiful," Edwina said. "And so . . . unworried."

Hepzibah began transferring dough back

into the bowl. "Children don't need to know what they can't understand. Grown-ups either," she added meaningfully.

"What about you? Aren't you worried about Hallie? She's been gone three days now."

"My feelings aren't any help one way or the other, are they? But if you want to know, I think anyone who'd try to keep that child away from here — well, they'd wind up with plenty more on their hands than they bargained for, that's all."

She set the bowl at the back of the range and covered it with a linen towel. "Here," she said, opening a drawer and removing a large book, "you'll see why."

Edwina reached out, found the pain in her chest replaced by a dull ache. The book was a leatherbound photo album. Hallie on a roller coaster whose dizzying height made Edwina's spine tingle. Braids flying, arms upthrust, eyes alight. Hallie clinging one-handed to a knotted rope, swinging out over a pond, forty feet at least to the water's glinting surface. Hallie with a huge furry spider crouched on her palm, her face intent as she peered at it.

Hepzibah watched Edwina turn the pages. "He says it's her scare book, Mr. Dietz does. She tells him all the things that make her afraid, and then they do them, and he takes a picture of it. To trap the fear, she says, so it can't get out of the picture. That child went to New York on the train alone when she was six, flew to California when she was seven. She wants to parachute jump, but she has to wait until she's big enough to fit the rig."

Hepzibah wiped her hands on a towel. "Wouldn't surprise me she showed up here tonight."

Edwina examined the photographs again before rising to hand the book back. The wine's muzzy kick had faded, and Hepzibah looked impatient to begin preparing Rebecca's dinner.

"She does look quite fearless."

"No," Hepzibah shook her head, "you don't understand. She's the timidest child, scared of everything. Like him, really," she added a little reluctantly. "But Mr. Dietz says — "

She held the towel in her hands and frowned, remembering. "He says being brave doesn't mean not being scared, it just means doing it anyway. And she's his little girl, so she believes him."

Satiated for once with activity and attention, Maxie trotted docilely behind her down the driveway. She stooped to smooth his fur, running her hand along the length of his body and closing it around the puff of soft hairs that collected on her fingers. When they reached the car he leapt inside, settling without protest into his carrying cage.

"Good boy." In the rearview mirror Hepzibah Scott stood sentry-like on the top step of the deck, watching as Edwina nosed the little car into the masses of scrub half-blocking the drive. She was still there, a small dark shape against the larger dark, when branches closed over the rear window.

To make sure I'm leaving, Edwina thought, waiting until the Fiat's tires bumped onto the blacktop before stopping to switch on the passenger-compartment light.

In her hand were thirty or forty of Maxie's short black cat hairs and a single long wavy one. She had noticed it clinging to him in the kitchen as she was readying herself to leave, its auburn glint showing against his jet-black coat.

Hepzibah's salt-and-pepper hair was tightly curled, trimmed very short and close to her small, finely shaped head. Rebecca's was neither as long as the one Edwina held nor as straight.

Hallie's hair was like this: long, dark, gently spiral waved from being constantly in braids.

Of course, Maxie could have picked this hair up anywhere — from under a bed, perhaps — except that to judge by Hepzibah's downstairs housekeeping there were no stray hairs under any of the Dietzes' beds, any more than there were dust balls or dirty dishes or grimy handprints anywhere in their house. The place was immaculate.

And Rebecca had stolen a second apple.

Speeding toward town, Edwina sorted her thoughts.

First: something someone didn't want known, something even Bill Claymore — a womanizer but one who at least didn't abandon his women — balked at revealing after his investigators learned of it.

Next: Maggie Dietz's art career, never mentioned or hinted at, ended — to judge by the truncated row of gallery posters and Hallie's birthdate — about the time her daughter was conceived.

Finally: Hepzibah Scott, and the problem of getting a child from a hospital lobby unnoticed.

Only Edwina no longer thought this posed a problem. Hallie Dietz knew the black woman well and would do what she said without question — had done so tonight in fact, waiting silently upstairs while Edwina sat below.

And the fall from the deck steps had been no accident. Gingerly, Edwina pressed her hand against her breastbone and was rewarded with a thump of pain.

Hepzibah had tripped her, she was sure of it.

The question was why?

"Can you believe it?" Holly asked, "he's still that cheap? Some kind of gentleman farmer now from what I hear, doctoring his family at a — "

"All three?" Edwina interrupted. She stood at a pay phone outside a Shell station. Inside, a chunky guy in grease-stained overalls was hauling the spare tire out of the Fiat's trunk.

She had, she decided upon spotting the station and the eighteen-wheelers barreling down Route 8, pushed her luck in that department far enough.

In several departments, actually; she had buzzed her phone machine at home, too. Six messages, five of them McIntyre's; he himself, however, was nowhere to be found.

"Uh-huh," Holly said. "Kid's vaccinations, couple of small things — chicken pox, flu — and one big thing, a bad burn."

"Right, I know about that. How far back do the records go?"

"Way back. Theirs are almost the only ones that do. Guess they didn't want to go through the witness thing again, or — "

"Witness thing?"

"Jehovah's Witnesses," said Holly as if Ed-

206

wina ought to have known it all along. "Anyway, that's what it says on the outside of all their charts. When people are, the records clerk sticks it on the chart so no one gives 'em a transfusion without them makin' a big deal out of it first, which is a waste of time because mostly when push comes to shove people take the transfusion."

"Right," Edwina broke in. "What about fertility checks on him? Sperm count, motility tests, anything like that?"

"Nope." Holly's voice turned smug. "On her, yes. But on him, just a note — declines further work-up. Lots of guys are like that, you know, got their manhood all tied up in their —"

"I guess," said Edwina, trying to keep disappointment from her voice.

"There is one other thing, though. Answers your question, too, I'll bet. Oliver Dietz," Holly said triumphantly, "had mumps. Real sick with 'em — stiff neck, high fever — when he was twenty-two. They nearly sent him down to Chelsea."

"Really," said Edwina. Adults got sicker with mumps than children did, but that was not why it was serious for men. In males past puberty, mumps often caused sterility.

The gas-station guy looked up grinning as she entered the station. "Good thing you stopped. You know this was here?"

He held a sliver of metal about four inches long. "It was sticking between the treads, could've let go any second."

"From the flat?" Up on the rack, the Fiat looked small and undignified.

"Nope. One you was running on. Wanna fix these? Other one, I could get ya home on it anyway."

She looked at him, knowing already what she was going to do and why. "What do you think?"

The gas-station guy got up, wiping his hands down the side of his pants. The red-and-white oval patch on his breast pocket said his name was Al.

"Lady," Al said, "if you was my wife, I'd buy ya two brand-new tires. You prob'ly think I'm just tryin' to sell 'em to ya, but that's what I'd do."

Edwina smiled. "You know what, Al? If I was my wife, I'd buy me two new tires, too. Put them on, will you, please?"

Which was how the last piece came.

"Damn!" The tire iron clanged to the floor as Al Turigiano sprang to his feet, cradling his hand.

Edwina got up from the old swivel chair by the cash register and walked past the soda machine, a rack of wiper inserts and the Pennzoil display to slide open the grease-smudged glass partition.

The garage smelled sweetly of tools and transmission fluid, antifreeze, crankcase oil and powdered soap. "You all right?"

"Yeah." He waved disgustedly. "Be done couple minutes."

She opened the dividing door and went in, ignoring a sign that read Due to Insurance Rules Customers Not Allowed in Shop. A drop of blood, then another, fell to the grease-blackened floor.

"Nah," he held his hand away. "This ain't, this's just a scratch. Get 'em all the time."

He'd sliced it a good three inches from the end of his left index finger to the knuckle joint. Deep, bleeding briskly, the gaping skin edges pale white.

"You get scratches like that all the time," she said, "you must make a lot of trips to the emergency room. I can tell you right now it's going to take three or four stitches to close."

"Christ," Al scowled. "You a doctor?"

"Nurse." She reached out; when he didn't jerk away she closed her fingers on his wrist, drawing the injured hand gently nearer. "Bleeding good, probably all nice and clean in there."

Which was partly true, but this blood spurted brightly and in time with his pulse. "Bend it, can you?"

He could: full range of motion. "Hurt?"

"Like the dickens," he admitted.

"Had a tetanus booster lately?"

His lip bulged. "Aw, not a shot, I'm a baby about shots."

"And I'm a baby about my friends getting lockjaw. How about I wrap this for you and you take it right on down to your local health-care professional? In fact, how about closing up now and I'll drive you there?"

He remained unconvinced as the lift brought the Fiat slowly down and she pulled the first-aid kit from beneath the seat. Bacitracin, a couple of tongue depressors, gauze squares, a roll of adhesive tape.

"Hey, you're pretty good at this," he said hopefully as she wrapped the finger. "Don'tcha think this'll do the trick?"

"Al." She pointed at the red stain seeping through.

"Oh." His face fell. "Ok then, I guess."

Edwina backed the Fiat off the lift tracks, wedged Maxie in back and got out to pull down the big garage doors while Al moved about inside, snapping off switches, locking locks.

"Lucky you drove in when you did,

though," he said as they pulled out, "you'da maybe had a flat on the way home, got stuck."

Very lucky, because she had already been stuck. But now in her mind's eye she saw blood: drops on a garage floor.

Tubes drawn and ready for testing.

Streaks, and then so much more, at the end of Grace's life.

And bags of it: units stamped with type and cross-match codes. Donated blood, for transfusions.

The kind Hallie Dietz couldn't receive, because her religion didn't permit transfusions — except under one special circumstance: she could bank her own blood, store it to be transfused back in surgery. For a child, that took time; a child's blood volume was smaller than an adult's. You couldn't draw off much at once.

Skin-graft surgery, though, could require a lot. So they'd have started banking early: labeled bags, stacked on the shelves of a blood-bank refrigerator.

Bags that might be there, Edwina thought, right this very minute.

TEN

"That," said McIntyre tightly, "is a nice idea. Too bad it won't work."

By the time Edwina arrived home the answering-machine score had risen to seven, all but one from McIntyre and all his calls sounding angry.

Not any angrier than he was right now, though. She didn't think it possible to be any angrier than McIntyre was now — not, at any rate, without suffering a cerebral hemorrhage as a result.

He had been at her door in ten minutes; inside, he refused a chair, a drink, and all her efforts to placate him, delivering instead the twenty-cent lecture on the topic of how he didn't need her help, didn't want her help, and if he did need help, dammit, he could get a hell of a lot more of it with a hell of a lot less irritation just by consulting a medical dictionary — mainly because when you looked for one of those it wasn't off racketing around by itself somewhere, asking a lot of questions and getting itself into a lot of damn-fool trouble.

"So," she asked when he paused for breath, "why won't it work?"

He stared. "You're not even going to apologize. Jesus, you could have been lying dead somewhere."

She folded her arms. "I'm not lying dead, though, am I?" It was not the politic moment to reveal her porch tumble. "I'm right here. I've brought back a motive, and now I'm looking to check that motive out. So why don't you cut to the chase?"

And that, she thought, will be that. She had insulted his manhood, alienated the living hell out of him, and as good as told him she could do his job as well as he could, which wasn't even true.

On the other hand, she added to herself, if you're going to be a stone bitch you might as well be up-front about it. Truth in advertising and all that.

Which was when he began to laugh, as apparently he was more easily amused than insulted, alienated, or threatened; always a good sign, she thought.

"You," he managed, "get right to the point, don't you? I'll take that drink now."

She brought the icy glass and sat across from him with her own. "You haven't said yet why my idea's a bust."

"Don't worry, I will. But first a deal —

next time you go hip-deep in something, you let me know you're going to, dammit."

She opened her mouth to protest; he held up a warning hand. "No, don't go getting your nose all out of joint. I know what you're thinking, and you're wrong."

He looked thoughtfully at his glass. "What I want to know is, how would you like it if the shoe had been on the other foot?"

"That's not — "

"Shut up, I'm not finished. What if I dropped out of sight and I might be in trouble? You care? Or you figure hey, what the hell, hardly know the guy. Forget it."

Edwina looked down. "You're taking this rather personally, aren't you?"

"Right. I get to like a person, I like to be sure some bastard hasn't stuffed them in a culvert. I'm funny that way. But hey, that's OK, you don't have to answer now. I've got time."

She shrugged. "It was inconsiderate of me. I apologize for worrying you."

"Also," he said, "I've got radios, cars, friendly judges who write me little notes, get me in places — not to mention guns, and not that you needed any of that. It's just I'd have liked to know I could use them is all."

He put his glass down. "In case," he added carefully, "you ever asked me for my help.

Unlikely as I'm sure that sounds to you, me being just a dumb cop and all."

"All right, don't rub it in. I get the picture." As she spoke she glared at him with grudging respect; it had been a long time since anyone made her feel this much of a jerk.

And been right, damn it.

"Yeah." He looked skeptical. "Maybe you do, we'll see. Anyway, the thing is, I thought the same as you when I started going through the kid's medical history, found out they've been banking her blood. Why not check out some of that, right? Find out whatever it is someone wants to hide so badly. Only blood doesn't keep that long — not the kind of blood we want, anyway."

Edwina raised her eyebrows. "The kind we want?"

"Whole blood," he ticked off, "forty-two days. Packed red cells the same, refrigerated, and some rare kinds they freeze, but that's out of our ballpark. Tissue typing, that's white cells, refrigeration kills 'em and they don't store them, anyway, except platelets. They last twenty-four hours, but that's not the right kind of white cell, is it?"

"Impressive," she remarked. "You're learning your way around fast."

He eyed her. "Took me half a day to find out what you could have told me in ten min-

215

utes. Ever hear of a little thing called division of labor? Folks who do things efficiently say they really like it. Besides, if you're right about the girl being in Albemarle, we won't need to test stored blood."

"You haven't sent someone up there? But I left you a — "

He shook his head. "No sense stirring up two hornet's nests at once. If she's there, it sounds like she's in a good, safe spot. And we don't know that whoever took her is our main man, do we? Or our main woman."

"I suppose," she said slowly, "someone who didn't do the murders could have taken her just as easily as somebody who did, but — " She looked at him. "What do you mean, two hornet's nests? What did you do when you found out the stored blood idea wasn't going to work?"

He grinned. "I called up the Claymores and Dietzes and told them it would. Hey," he spread his hands innocently, "my mistake. So I'm no medical expert, so sue me."

Edwina stared. Team play with this guy might be fun; too bad he'd just fouled out. "You what?"

McIntyre looked smug. "Uh-huh. Implied it would anyway. I invited them to a meeting, said I knew they'd want to hear the great progress I was making with the help of modern science and all. Of course, I didn't say it was science *fiction*."

"To see who does something weird."

"That's right, because one of them's a liar. Not to mention a murderer, and it's starting to make me mad. So now Talbot's in a car, watching outside the Holiday Inn, and I snagged a helper to sit outside the Ramada, and — "

She got up. "What time is the meeting supposed to be?"

He glanced at his watch. "Eight. At Chelsea Memorial in an hour, in a conference room on the — hey, what's up?"

That's why she did it, Edwina thought, tripped me and got me inside, kept me sitting there. Not to tell me something; just to make me think she might. Stalling for time.

Grabbing her bag, coat, and keys, she shooed him toward the door. "You didn't let me finish. You had to yell first, get it all off your chest."

"Oh, come on, you were gone one day. What else — "

"You didn't let me *finish*. No one needs to go anywhere, they'll bring Hallie here. And then they'll — "

"Who? Who's bringing her?"

In the hall she hammered the elevator button, swore, grabbed his elbow, and urged him toward the stairwell door.

"Hepzibah Scott," she said.

"I went out to the c-convenience store," Oliver Dietz said. "When I got buh-back — "

He shook his head in disbelief. "She wouldn't let me in. And Hallie was there."

They'd found him on the street in front of the hotel; now he sat in the coffee shop, McIntyre on one side and Edwina on the other.

"She said if I tried to get back in the ruh-room, she'd . . . she'd hurt me." His eyes expressed wounded shock. "Hallie too, and herself. Or if anyone else tried, so puh-please don't — "

"No one will," McIntyre said grimly. "How did your wife know when you'd be out of the way?"

Dietz's forehead furrowed. "The ph-phone rang. She said it was a wrong n-number. That must have been when — "

Edwina nodded. "Hepzibah, calling the second time — from right outside the hotel."

"I should have t-told her it didn't m-matter. I love them buh-both, I would never have — "

"What?" She turned to him. "What didn't matter?"

Fighting tears, he raised his face. "Hallie's not mine. I wouldn't do the tests when we were trying to get puh-pruh — when we were trying to have her. But later I wuh-went and had them done my muh-myself."

His face twisted. "I cuh-can't have kids, but I p-pretended not to know. If nobody said it, it wasn't ruh-real. And then I forgot about it. As good as, anyway."

A sob escaped him. "It was in the past," he forced the words out, "but now she was staying home and we were huh-happy.

"Only," he added miserably, "Maggie was afraid, I guh-guess. She was going to run away, after she . . . when she couldn't stop the tests. Run away from muh-*me*."

McIntyre frowned. "What did you mean about Hepzibah calling here the second time?"

"The first time," Edwina explained, "was the minute she saw me pull into the Dietzes' driveway, to find out what to do about me. And that got Maggie into gear even more than she was."

"I don't get it," McIntyre said, and Dietz looked puzzled too.

"She thought time was running out because she believed what you said, Martin, about your progress. Maybe she even thought you knew it all already, that you were going to pull one of those unmasking-the-culprit stunts at the meeting you'd called them all to attend."

"I don't see how you could make it any

worse for her, then," McIntyre objected.

"Oh, but I could. I could get seriously in her way, because she knew if I saw her textiles, *I'd* know she wasn't the simple country wife she'd been posing as — to everyone. Remember you said the Dietzes might look a little thick, but they weren't?"

Dietz grimaced but had no strength to protest.

"Well," she went on, "I should have kept that in mind. But when I saw that studio and what was in it, I knew — there was plenty more to Maggie than she'd let on and plenty more to her story. The dates on the posters were the key, and she knew once I saw them I'd come back here and want to talk to her right away."

Not to accuse her of murder; there'd still been too many loose ends for that. But now no accusations were necessary, were they? Maggie had taken care of that herself.

She turned to Dietz. "Did you lay down an ultimatum — no more shows, no more solitary travel? No more temptations? Or was that a punishment she put on herself for getting involved with another man while she was away and for getting pregnant by him?"

Dietz flushed. "I tuh-told you . . . I never s-said anything."

Before Albemarle she might have believed

him. But now she'd seen the scary book, the record of his terrifying challenges to a fearful child.

She brings him things that scare her, Hepzibah had said, but looking at Oliver Dietz's reddened, stubborn face Edwina was willing to bet it was more the other way around. Only Hallie'd kept calling his bluff, beating every fear he threw at her and coming back for more, believing it was for her good.

Which maybe it was, now. Odds were, Hallie Dietz was going to need all her bravery, however this night worked out.

"No matter," she said, turning back to McIntyre. "Thing is, she didn't have time to talk with me, play the innocent. She needed the time she had left to get ready whatever she's got in mind. And whatever it is includes Hallie, so Hepzibah brought her down and sneaked her in somehow. No one was watching people going in, after all, only going out."

McIntyre's face hardened. "Maybe I ought to go and have a word with the indispensable Ms. Scott. They picked her up on her way back up there," he added. "Says she doesn't know anything, didn't do anything. Hear her tell it, she barely exists."

"You can try, but she won't say anything that might hurt Maggie. Although I do think Maggie took advantage of that, because

Hepzibah wouldn't deliberately put Hallie in danger either."

She looked at McIntyre. "So now what?"

"Well, she says she's got a gun, and history suggests she's telling the truth — about that, anyway. And that she's capable of using it."

He looked unhappy. "That leaves us two choices. Get her to come out or go in after her. Crazy lady holed up with a gun and a little girl, I can tell you right now it won't be long before I get an order from upstairs — go to plan B."

In the mirror on the far side of the counter, Edwina watched the hotel manager arguing furiously with a pair of uniformed men. About plan B, probably.

"I thought hostage situations could go on for hours."

"Not when the taker's got a history of hurting people," he replied. "Especially not when the hostage is a child."

Talbot came into the coffee shop, caught McIntyre's eye, and motioned him over. "Be right back," he said.

"What's going to happen now?" Dietz asked.

"I don't know," Edwina told him. In the mirror, Talbot and McIntyre debated something, glanced at Edwina, and argued some more.

"You didn't," she asked Dietz, "really switch them somehow? The babies — when Maggie was unconscious after the cesarean, you didn't think a sick baby might be too hard for you? Or that it might hurt Maggie's art somehow, or — "

Someone at the clinic might simply have approached him with a suggestion, veiled at first and then explicit; it was how the others had been done.

"No," he replied, shocked. "There really was another b-baby, only no one believes it."

From the corner of her eye she caught McIntyre's summoning look and crossed to where the officers stood.

"I don't like it," McIntyre was saying, "I just don't — "

"She wants to talk to you," Talbot said. "They got her on the phone, she said she'd let you in. Alone."

"How did she sound?"

"Pretty snarled up. I'd go but she's not having any."

"Did they talk to the little girl?"

He shook his head. "They said they could hear her crying, though. They think she's OK."

Edwina's eyes met Dietz's briefly in the mirror. "But why?"

The two men looked at her. "I mean," she

went on, "what is the big deal about all of this? If we've got it right, what's going to come out — what the blood tests would have shown — is that Oliver isn't Hallie's father. But he knows that already, so why would she kill to try to hide it?"

"If she didn't," McIntyre said, "why's she doing this?"

"Maybe," Talbot suggested, "she didn't know he knew?"

She frowned, trying to remember precisely what Oliver Dietz had said. "Maybe," she said doubtfully. "Did anybody ask her?"

"I don't have to ask anybody anything to know that this is nuts," McIntyre said. "You can't go, you don't know what you'll say to her once you get inside or what she'll do."

The elevator stood at the end of a corridor off the lobby. "Right, life's just full of little challenges."

She stopped before the open doors. "Look, in my business I deal with plenty of scared people, sometimes even angry people. It'll be all right."

Privately she wished she felt as confident as she sounded. Still . . .

"Right now Maggie's scared. She feels trapped. She thinks she's got no options — so I'll give her some, and she'll pick one. She's got to know she can't stay up there forever."

"She's killed two people. One was a friend of yours."

Edwina closed her eyes a moment. "Martin, I got into this because Julia asked me to. I went on with it partly for revenge — I wanted to catch whoever'd done it, hurt them back. And," she confessed, "to impress you a little bit, I guess."

His eyebrows went up.

"But," she went on, "right now I'm not here for revenge, or as anyone's friend. Or to impress you. I'm here as a professional person, a nurse."

She looked at him. "See, every nurse prays for two things — first, that she'll never be in the kind of trouble she sees every day. But mostly she prays that if she ever is, there'll be another nurse there, a good one who'll try to help her instead of making a lot of judgments about how she got into trouble in the first place. And what goes around comes around, see?"

Smiling, she tried to make her voice light. "So call her, why don't you? Tell her I said please don't shoot me."

He hesitated, then gave in. "There's two stairwells, one at either end of the hall. Guys're already there, so you need help, you yell for it."

He blocked the door with his shoe. "How

you going to handle her?"

"Try to remember my psych nursing, hope she's a textbook case."

"Yeah. OK, I guess. See you shortly. Don't screw up."

She made a face at him as the doors slid finally shut, then sagged against the walnut contact paper lining the elevator car. Hey, she thought, imitating his voice in her head — you talk the talk, you've got to walk the walk, right?

You twit, she added as the doors slid open.

The carpet on the fourth floor was olive green, the walls beige fake burlap. Somewhere an ice machine hummed. The air had a stale, faintly plastic used-up smell.

Edwina scanned for the room number, saw one door opening a crack. "Maggie? It's me, Edwina."

Rule one for dealing with patients of any stripe: always take the time to identify yourself.

Good rule, but Maggie hadn't read the book. In the space between door and frame, a small blue circle appeared.

Edwina stopped. Be aware that the patient's sense of his or her own personal space may be distorted and that invasion of it may be perceived as threatening.

"Don't point the weapon at me, please. If

you do, I'll have to leave — and I won't be able to come back."

Speak calmly and firmly. Explain what you want and what the consequences will be if your request is ignored.

The small blue circle disappeared.

"Good. I'm coming in now." Describe what you are about to do in detail. "I'm going to open the door and come inside."

No answer. From within the room came the sound of a child crying. "Here I come. Take it easy."

The door slammed shut.

Damn. "Hey, I didn't call you, you know. Open the door, unless you've changed your mind. I'll count to five."

Provide clear limits. ". . . five."

The door swung wide. The room was a cave, draperies drawn and no lamps burning. This little drama was Maggie's revenge, her punishment for the way Edwina had messed up all her plans.

I hope. She stepped in and the door swung shut. In the darkness, the little girl's voice came from somewhere to her right.

Crying harder now, muffled and echoing. In the bathroom with the door closed, maybe locked.

"Maggie, will you turn on a light, please?"

Always be polite, even when the patient has

murdered two people in cold blood.

Especially then, actually.

A lamp snapped on. Maggie Dietz sat on the far bed, wearing a red cotton jacket, blue shirt, navy slacks. Beside her lay a small travel bag and a large tan cloth purse. In both her large smooth hands she gripped a .22 target pistol.

Also on the bed lay a pair of airline tickets in folders, torn raggedly in half.

"May I sit down?" Edwina crossed to the chair by the window.

"No," Maggie snapped. "Here, where I can see you."

The sobbing grew frantic. "She sounds scared. Can't we get her out of here? You and I could stay."

Maggie frowned. "She'll stay. She's obedient, Hallie is. And I want her with me."

"I see." Edwina paused. "Oliver's downstairs. He's very concerned."

Maggie's head jerked up. "Where?"

"In the coffee shop. He asked me to tell you — "

"He didn't ask you to tell me anything, so don't say he did."

Never lie. They can smell it on you.

"Call them," Maggie said. Calm again; too calm. "Tell them to ring the coffee shop. That's where they are with my husband, right? The police?"

228

Edwina nodded. "When I get them, what should I say?"

Maggie sounded sure about her one-sentence answer, which Edwina repeated when McIntyre came on the line.

"Martin, she says she's going to kill me, then Hallie, then herself."

At this distance, the .22 looked big enough to hurt. Head, Edwina thought; lungs, liver, heart.

Over the past three hours there had been quiet murmurings, footsteps from the hall as other guests were hurried out, but now there was only silence.

No telephone; Maggie had yanked it after the dozenth try at reaching her from downstairs. Now she sat in a chair saying nothing, and the sounds from the bathroom had subsided, too; the little girl was probably asleep.

Maggie looked confident with her weapon. Tin cans, maybe, down on the farm. Shoulders loose, arms relaxed. Serene in her decision, which Edwina did not view as a good omen.

If Maggie shot her and managed to hit even a fair-sized artery, Edwina realized, she could bleed out very fast.

Distantly she wondered if an ambulance was already waiting and who was on call for emergency surgery tonight.

Please God, not Feinstein, that joker, and not Judd; he talks a good game but he can't make decisions. Wister, let it be Abby Wister, smart fingers and not afraid to cut.

And let the emergency room not be full of other traumas when I roll in. No six-car crack-ups on the turnpike, no drug deal gone sour on the Hill, no kid run over on his paper route. Let it go the way it should, please, after she shoots me.

Because she is going to shoot me, I don't know what she's waiting for but I can see it in her . . .

Eyes.

Wrong. Edwina frowned. "Maggie. What's the deal? Come on, talk to me."

Because her eyes were wrong. They weren't crazy pinwheels whirling on some illusory nothing, spinning to it. No huge dark pupils and not pinpoints either. Her hands weren't shaking, she didn't smell of fear-sweat, or of drink.

Sensorium intact, oriented times three; speech — what there was of it — lucid and appropriate.

If, Edwina thought, you could call her threat appropriate, which perhaps under the circumstances you could. The trouble was, the circumstances seemed suddenly unclear.

Hope she's a textbook case.

But she wasn't: no manic-depressive who'd given up taking her lithium, no schizophrenic flameout in thrall to voices only she could hear. No, Maggie was under control. Confident and smiling, because . . .

A burst of sudden nervousness made Edwina look away from that calm, controlled gaze to the bed and the airline tickets lying on it. Printed on the bottom half of each ticket folder was the flight number and the seating assignment: #229, seats D and F.

As long as no one said it, it wasn't ruh-real.

In the next moment she heard locks breaking, doorjambs splintering, men shouting. "No! No, she *isn't* going to . . . dammit, Maggie — drop!"

The door exploded in.

Edwina hurled herself at Maggie's hips, rolling hard across the bed to catch the other woman and take her down. But Maggie slid away. Edwina hit the floor, scrambled for Maggie's feet.

Two sharp explosions, or three. Maggie's mouth opened in protest as an invisible fist seemed to smack her, spinning her back.

One of the flak-jacketed men spied Edwina and fell on her. Another kicked the bathroom door, came out with the little girl struggling and shrieking in his arms. A third charged to where Maggie Dietz had fallen, crouching

231

by her and shouting for medical assistance.

Edwina felt herself half-marched and half-carried. The hallway was full of men: uniforms, suits, and more of the bulky dark-blue jackets the charging men had worn. The air stank of cordite and crackled with radio static. The ambulance techs came on at a sprint, carrying a stretcher and first-aid gear to where Maggie lay.

No McIntyre. Where the hell was he? Edwina searched the mass of faces, found Talbot's.

"Tell him!" she couldn't hear through the ringing in her ears. "Tell him not to — "

Talbot frowned, turning toward Edwina's voice, saw her and began pushing toward her. "What? I can't — "

She was babbling, tried to stop and couldn't. As he neared, Talbot's expression changed.

"Oh, shit," he said.

Something wet; warm heaviness in her chest. Pain, too; she couldn't be sure where. She followed Talbot's gaze.

"I'll be darned. She did it after all. She shot me."

The walls loomed and shrank away. A red stain was spreading fast on her shirt front. Horrified, she felt a giggle rising and bit down on it.

"Sit," Talbot ordered, and her legs folded obediently.

"Tell them," she managed, peering up into his face, which was now swelling and shrinking like the walls. "Tell them not to . . ."

"Take it easy," Talbot soothed. For a big man, his hands were remarkably gentle.

"You don't get it," she shouted, but her voice came out a squeak; sound was on the fritz entirely, her voice thinning out like a bell in a vacuum jar. She struggled against Talbot's arms, heard someone in the far distance yelling anxiously for medics.

Talbot, she thought, was looking quite alarmed; someone must have been hurt.

"Ticket," she whispered.

Talbot mouthed something; she strained to read his lips.

You're going to be just fine.

Yeah, sure, she thought. That's what they all say.

Then the lights went out.

She woke on her back on the angio table in the vascular radiology suite: very dim bluish lights, silver glow from the backlit film boards, and a nearer glow from the angiography screen.

By angling her eyes toward her toes, for she dared not move anything else, she could see the round screen. On it in dark relief against a bright gray background, the fine branchy structure of her own pulmonary vasculature was being displayed.

Into one of the branches snaked the dark tip of the angio catheter: advancing, hesitating, finding its way at last into the next smaller branch.

No pain, only a tugging at the side of her neck; arterial access, she realized, left subclavian.

On the screen, a puff of dye exploded from the end of the catheter like the sudden ink cloud of a disturbed squid. The ink spread.

Drat, she thought muzzily. From behind the lead screens came a low murmuring of voices.

". . . clip that off."

". . . is the room ready?"

". . . send up all eight units."

". . . tape that, or you want a stitch?"

". . . OK, let's go."

". . . two, three . . ."

". . . let's *go*."

ELEVEN

"A swordsman," drawled Harriet Crusoe, costumed as usual as formally as the Queen Mum: flowered navy silk dress, pale silk stockings, stacked-heeled navy pumps. Her big black purse and white gloves lay on the windowsill beside her wide-brimmed black felt hat from whose grosgrain ribbon a bunch of silk rosebuds bloomed discreetly. Around her neck she wore a rope of perfect, and perfectly enormous, pink-white heirloom pearls.

"Really," she pronounced, "how exceedingly quaint."

"But I don't see," objected Holly Ribolow, "why he would do such a silly thing — Claymore, I mean."

"Why, because he'd fallen in love with her, of course, during all those court hearings and so on. Or thought he had." Harriet looked up from the needlepoint canvas with which her plump manicured fingers were busily employed. "Edwina, dear, are you sure you wouldn't like to try this? Idle hands, you know."

Edwina opened her eyes. "Thank you, but

235

I really don't think I'll care for anything to do with yarns or fabrics for quite some time. Or to do with — ouch — stitches."

Five days had passed since what Harriet insisted upon calling "that terrible incident." During that time Edwina had been surgically opened and her contents given, it seemed, a vigorous stir, after which she had been sewn back together with what felt remarkably like pieces of rusty barbed wire.

A good deal of other therapeutic attention had been lavished upon her during those days, too, all of it, at least at first, quite urgently necessary and none of it pleasant, either to endure or to dwell upon.

"I don't suppose," she inquired faintly, "it's even nearly time for my pain medication yet?"

Being a patient in a hospital was bad enough; being one in the hospital where one was employed ought to be prohibited by law, for in front of one's friends it was nearly impossible not to be brave, cheerful, and cooperative when what one really longed for was to give out with a series of heartfelt groans, preferably while socking somebody in the jaw.

"What do you mean, in love?" Holly demanded, checking her wristwatch professionally and consulting her clipboard to see when Edwina's next dose might be due. "Why, he hardly knew her."

Oh, for heaven's sake, thought Edwina, it's only percocet. You'd think I was asking for heroin.

But Holly, so recently and abruptly restored to nursing respectability — as well as to the chance of earning a decent living for a change — wasn't about to neglect a single step in the serious routine of medicine giving.

"Indeed," Harriet said, "and that was his habit, wasn't it? Getting involved with women whom he hardly knew and into foolish and expensive difficulties thereby."

". . . getting ladies out of trouble he didn't help get them into," Phineas Quinn had said, "and if you believe that, you're even younger than you look."

But of course it was just what William Claymore had been doing, proving again how various and surprising people could be when they really put their minds to it.

William Claymore was not Hallie Dietz's father, but when he learned Oliver Dietz wasn't either, he tried to help Margaret Dietz out by hiding that fact. Edwina wondered if he was so used to helping women he had gotten into trouble that when he found out he hadn't, he simply did it automatically anyway.

Carefully, Holly shook two tablets from a bottle, read the label again thoroughly, then dropped the tablets into a medicine cup before pouring a glass of water with maddening slowness.

"Thank you," said Edwina, snatching at the tablets and gobbling them, gasping as the pills went down. The motion jarred her incision, which at the moment seemed to be made from bright shards of broken glass.

"You," Holly observed, "have a very low pain threshold."

"Right, and we'll see where yours is when I'm feeling a bit more fit, won't we?" Edwina shot back.

"Girls," Harriet murmured imperturbably. As it turned out she had not stopped at securing a Fitzwilliam place for Randy Ribolow, going on instead in her intensely interested way to investigate Holly's whole life — and then of course to fix it, the absence of a happy ending being one thing Harriet could not abide.

Precisely how Harriet had managed to get Holly's nursing license reinstated, Edwina didn't know and didn't care to inquire; she supposed that like trust funds, nursing licenses could be fiddled, and Holly did seem rehabilitated — perhaps, Edwina thought, even a bit too rehabilitated.

"A *chivalrous* man," Harriet said now, "but a terrible fool. Having long ago chosen respectability, he proceeded in his heart to adore precisely the opposite. And compared to that dim, shallow Jane, Maggie was not only a legitimate working artist, she was also a scarlet woman." She pronounced this last phrase as if tasting some small delicious tidbit. "And *that* was why he stole those court records — because he knew the dates in them would reveal Maggie's secret, eventually, in an open hearing. That she wasn't pregnant when she left for that last gallery show in Los Angeles — but that she was when she got back."

The meeting with his private investigators hadn't been to learn new information, of course; it had been to call them off.

Harriet smiled indulgently. "A martyr to romance — and of course an utter idiot, like most martyrs. Still, hardly knowing Maggie, he was actually preparing to drop the lawsuit, in spite of his wife's obsession and his own considerable financial interest in it."

Briskly, Holly finished straightening the bed linen. "You can't mean he and Maggie were planning to — "

"Oh, no, of course not. Don't you see? He loved her from afar." With a sharp little snick! that made Edwina wince, Harriet scissored off a piece of red yarn and threaded her needle with green.

"Not that Maggie would have responded if he had approached her. She was so under the

239

thumb of that truly regrettable husband of hers, that Oliver."

Harriet made a face. "Just imagine, ten years of silence and she so talented — what a little bully he was, behind that weak facade, and completely deluded, too."

She eyed Edwina. "And let that be a lesson to you, dear. Even a strong woman may have a fatal flaw — in poor Margaret's case I'm afraid it was the need to be helpful to someone."

She snipped another thread. "Personally, I've never found helpfulness all that fulfilling, but there you are. There's an ass," she finished tartly, "for every seat."

Edwina restrained a guffaw only by remembering that it would hurt. "You don't seem to mind being helpful lately," she observed, glancing at Holly.

Harriet glared. "A foolish consistency," she quoted, "is the hobgoblin of little minds. Don't you agree?"

"Yes, ma'am," Holly replied rather frightenedly, a thing Edwina had to admit did her heart good to see. Feeling her pain pills kicking in, she could see also that these two were going to get along famously.

Holly, it seemed, would be taking up residence at the farm in Litchfield when her stint of nursing Edwina was done, since Harriet maintained that old ladies always had need of nurses if only to prevent their needing doctors.

As if remembering this, Holly filled another water glass. "I think it's time for your own medication, Mrs. Crusoe," she said. "But I still don't understand — "

Harriet accepted the capsules Holly proffered with a resigned little moue. "Why did he do it? Why did Oliver Dietz kill those women and then let his wife attempt to accept the blame — long enough, at any rate, for him to escape?"

She popped the pills. "Because he didn't know Claymore was quietly preparing to drop the custody action. The two of them by then were of a single mind — to forestall courtroom revelations — but Claymore of course hadn't told Dietz. He hadn't decided that, himself, until the very last moment.

"And," she went on, "Dietz believed what he told Edwina. That if no one said a thing, it wasn't real. An all-too-common misapprehension, I'm afraid, and in his case also a thoroughly destructive one."

"He'd gone on for years," Edwina explained, "being little king, having things his own way. His wife," she recited, "had *not* been unfaithful, had *not* fallen out of love with him, was *not* stronger, more talented, more ambitious, and successful than he. His daughter was *not* someone else's child, and she was *not* afraid of spiders and high places, and — "

"Gad," Holly said. "Everything just ducky in Dietzworld, huh?"

Edwina blinked; Holly too, it seemed, could be surprising when she chose. "Exactly, only it was falling apart. The blood tests were going to show the truth to the whole world — the real world — and his perfect pretend world was going to fall down."

"Maggie could face that," Harriet put in, "but he couldn't, and he also couldn't look as if he had anything to fear. He simply denied it all, even to himself — until he panicked and stopped the blood tests the only way he knew how. By murder."

"And Maggie," Edwina said, "sacrificed herself for him one last time. She knew he'd done it the minute it happened, she'd known all along he knew about Hallie — she simply knew him too well. She gave him an alibi, got hold of the plane tickets, told him they'd all make a run for it. Not that it could have worked. Besides, I put a wrench in those monkeyworks, so at last she provoked a crisis to give him a chance to try alone — insisting to him and to herself that he could manage it. Which, of course, he couldn't."

She sank back to the pillow. "Poor Maggie," she finished. "If she hadn't had Hepzibah all

242

those years, he'd probably have driven her nuts — maybe even as nuts as he was himself."

The only thing worse than a hospital bed was the long slow process of clambering painfully out of one, especially for a person whose important body parts felt held together with adhesive tape.

Still, having to ask for help with the simplest things was pretty painful too, and the wheelchair was only a few feet away. Gripping the side rail, Edwina eased nearer the bed's edge. To her surprise, her insides remained inside.

"There she goes," Martin McIntyre said from the doorway, "taking off again without bothering to let anyone know."

Beyond him the corridor was dim and silent; it was long past visiting hours, Holly's shift was done, and even Harriet had finally gone home. Edwina, who had been looking forward to a few hours of privacy, noted that McIntyre's presence did not disturb this luxury. On the contrary, actually.

"Hello," she said. "What are you doing here?"

He was hiding something rather clumsily behind his back. "Someone I thought you might like to see," he said. "How about hopping up to that chair first."

It wasn't a question, and the phrase "hopping up" didn't even begin to describe what Edwina did. Hauling her legs out of bed was a project in itself, while standing on her own two feet was an event deserving applause and cheers.

A few steps away the wheelchair seemed to glow faintly like some low-budget but still extremely desirable version of Shangri-la. Edwina tottered toward it, clinging to her wheeled IV pole with one hand while grabbing at the gaping back of her hospital-issue gown with the other.

Gasping and furious at her own continuing wobbliness, she sank into the chair. "Excellent," pronounced McIntyre. "You really are looking remarkably well. Considering, I mean."

"Liar." Still, it felt good hearing it. "Why have you been avoiding me? I've been out of ICU two days."

Not that she had wanted to see anyone, or have anyone see her. Wrath of God was putting it mildly compared to what she looked like: skinny, green, and on the brink of death. Which was where she had been, she thought wonderingly, hard as that fact still was to believe or to comprehend.

"I was there," he said, kindly making light of it, "before you began recuperating. Since then I've been out hunting up the proper present to celebrate. And it took a little doing . . ."

Turning, he fiddled with whatever it was he'd put down on the floor, then turned back with a cat in his arms.

"Maxie." Ignoring the pain she reached out for the animal who reached out companionably in return and settled in her arms at once, butting his black-velvet head against her chin.

"Maxie, you beast, I am awfully glad to see you."

Probably he was a dreadful infection hazard and his weight on her stomach really was rather painful, but she didn't care; suddenly she didn't feel nearly so ill as she had.

"Oh, thank you. How did you ever get him in here?"

"Prutt," Maxie said, gazing contentedly up at her with his strange yellow-slit feline eyes.

"The doorman let me into your place," McIntyre explained, "and Mrs. Friedlander felt the rules could be bent just this once. A sort of reward, seeing as . . ." He stopped uncomfortably.

"Seeing," she finished for him, "as Julia's decided not to retire after all, so her job won't be opening up for me to walk into. It's all right, I'd decided not to take it anyway."

"Really?" He tipped his head enquiringly.

Maxie squirmed, sniffing at the medicine smells on her skin. "Really. I've decided to change careers. After all, I have a perfectly good brain and more money than anyone deserves. I can do," she finished, "anything I want to do."

Amazing how sharp a reminder the point of death could be, actually, especially when aimed however temporarily at oneself.

McIntyre stared. "You mean you're quitting nursing?"

"Oh, no," she laughed, "certainly not. Private duty — only not with agencies. I'm going to start my own agency for . . . unusual cases. Confidential kinds of cases, you see."

He nodded. "Yes, I suppose I do see. And how, may I ask, do you expect to find these cases?"

She returned his look evenly. "Oh, I think I'm apt to get referrals, once word gets around. Quiet word, as soon as I'm healed a little more. Speaking of which — "

"Edwina, I'm sorry. I told them you'd have it all under control, but it was out of my hands. They had to have their dramatic rescue," he finished bitterly.

His eyes really were the palest gray, the color of a foggy morning. "I knew that. But thank you for saying it anyway. I did trust you, Martin, really, I knew you wouldn't . . . do you know your face is remarkably expressive? Especially," she added, feeling a trifle breathless, "when it's so very near?"

"Yes, as a matter of fact I do know that," said McIntyre, coming nearer still.

"But you can't," began the unhappy young police officer stationed outside Maggie Dietz's hospital room.

"Oh, of course I can," Edwina said, watching with approval as two burly aides lifted Maggie from her bed. Gently they deposited her in a wheelchair that was the twin of Edwina's.

"After all," she told the policeman, who looked barely old enough to be packing a cap gun, much less that enormous special revolver, "she's not much of an escape risk at the moment, is she?"

She observed with approval the aides raising Maggie's arm, steel pinned and heavily casted, to its prescribed position and adjusting the stockinette sling around it. The police bullet had shattered her elbow, inflicting quite a lot of nerve damage; still, she was expected to get back most of it — someday.

"Besides," said Edwina, "this trip is medically necessary." Which was not quite a lie, good mental health being crucial to medical recovery according to all the experts, chief among whom at the moment Edwina counted herself.

"Ready?" she called.

Maggie managed a frightened smile. "Ready," she whispered as the aides wheeled her from the room.

Her mouse-colored hair had been washed and brushed, the nails of her good hand trimmed and coated with polish, her pale lips touched lightly with pink. She was silent as they rolled along, Edwina self-propelled and Maggie pushed by the young policeman who still seemed to feel she might make a break for it.

"What," she whispered when they had maneuvered into an elevator, "if she doesn't want to see me?"

Edwina turned in surprise. "Maggie, of course she'll want to see you — you're her mother, for heaven's sake."

But Maggie only smiled worriedly, shrugging as best she could. "They told me she was quite upset."

Which was an understatement. After one night in emergency foster care, Hallie Dietz had been admitted to Chelsea's inpatient Kids at Risk program, where she continued manifesting night terrors, bed wetting, thumb sucking, and loss of language skills — infantile behaviors of the most inauspicious kind. All she wanted was for everything to be as it had been — which was, of course, precisely all that she couldn't have.

Oliver Dietz had been seized at Union Station trying to get on a train. He hadn't resisted arrest and when confronted with Maggie's injury had broken down entirely, admitting all. Now he awaited arraignment for the deaths of Helene Motavalli and Grace Savarin on charges of first-degree murder.

The elevator doors let them out past several small labs and clinic waiting areas and down a hall that smelled of formalin and rubbing alcohol toward the Peters-Darrows Medical Auditorium. From behind big wooden double doors came music and the sounds of children laughing.

"The Claymores found their baby," Maggie said. "Mr. Claymore telephoned my attorney this morning and said he thought I'd like to know."

Edwina blinked. "But — how?"

"The other baby's mother read in the newspapers about what happened at the hotel. She's the clinic director's daughter, of all people — the one who killed himself, remember?"

"Of course," Edwina breathed. "So that's what happened."

Maggie nodded. "She was only fifteen, but she insisted on keeping it — so when he saw

249

it was sick, he switched that baby with the Claymores' and that's how it all began. Later the girl figured out what must have happened, but by that time her father was dead — she didn't know what to do, so she did nothing. Besides, she really did love the baby, hers or not."

"So why speak up now?"

"Because," Maggie said sadly, "now she's living on welfare in Hartford, can't put decent clothes on the child or feed her decent food. She's offering to share custody if the Claymores help her get back on her feet."

"I see," said Edwina, and then she spotted Martin McIntyre striding down the corridor toward them.

Maggie saw him too. "You tricked me," she said dully, the little color she had draining from her face. "He's going to try to — "

"No, he's not." This was the part Edwina hadn't been able to plan in detail: how Maggie might react. "He's trying to help you and so am I. You don't have to say a thing."

Maggie turned away stonily. "Why should you help me? I'm the one who shot you, remember?"

"Right. Viciously, on purpose. With malice aforethought you took that gun and you aimed it straight at me, and you — "

"No." Maggie moved her body clumsily

250

back to face Edwina. "No, the bullet hit my elbow and the gun went off, I never — oh."

She eyed Edwina cautiously as the realization struck her. "When the nerves — my hand clenched shut on its own. There'll be medical evidence of that, won't there?"

Hope brightened in her face as McIntyre neared her chair, which stopped alongside Edwina's before the auditorium doors.

"That's right," he said. "No intent. I just talked with the prosecutors — you're going to be charged with reckless endangerment, accessory after the fact, conspiring to obstruct, and filing a false report. Oh, and the weapons charge."

The young policeman looked impressed but remained silent.

"Not," McIntyre emphasized, "with endangering the welfare of a child — they could, but if they did you'd probably never get Hallie back. Which," he added, "I have to tell you, you still might not."

"But I might," she said, "if — what?"

Swiftly McIntyre told her, not omitting the bad parts or soft-pedaling any of the difficulties. The upshot was that if Maggie agreed to testify she would get immunity, while Oliver would be allowed to plead to lesser charges.

As Maggie listened her rejecting look faded,

changing to a series of thoughtful nods; when the double doors opened and the two wheelchairs rolled in, she turned back to Edwina.

"What do you think?" she asked.

"I think," Edwina replied, "you don't have a choice. If you don't, he could get — "

But Maggie was no longer listening, for a little girl with long dark braids was running toward her, arms open wide.

"Good lord," said McIntyre, cautiously wheeling Edwina's chair into the fray, "are you sure these are sick children?"

The din really was astonishing. Some of the kids wore the yellow-and-blue cotton hospital-issue gowns; a few, bandaged or in body casts, lay on stretchers covered only by blankets and sheets. IV poles, medication pumps, casts and tractions and wheelchairs warred for space among the red and blue child-size chairs and tables, while youngsters unencumbered by devices scrambled, shouted, and ran.

"They don't get to cut loose much," she said. "I guess they're taking advantage of the chance."

To one side of the big old room, a refreshment table had been set up, and nurses were doling out portions of cookies, milk, and fruit juice. Up on the big stage a dozen older children and teenagers milled impatiently, all wearing togas made of sheets and belted with IV tubing, foam hospital-issue slippers cut to resemble sandals, and wreaths of plastic greenery on their heads.

One, a pale slender girl in a wheelchair, also wore an oxygen mask; behind it she was smiling and saying something to a tall, dark-haired boy whose arm ended in a metal prosthesis. A red paper heart was pinned to the girl's toga; the boy pointed to it and said something, and they laughed. Edwina thought the girl looked familiar but couldn't think why.

"Feel like taking a little nourishment?" McIntyre asked, nodding at the bar. "Grape juice and ginger ale?"

She nodded, catching sight of Jim Lobrutto hurrying over.

"I still don't understand how they managed it," Lobrutto said, looking even more than usual like a movie star miscast in the role of cleric. "How did they get her away without anybody seeing her? Out of the hospital lobby, I mean."

Edwina shifted in the chair, winced, and shifted deliberately again. If she was going to get out of this place ahead of schedule as she intended she'd better get used to some pain.

"Simple," she told him. "Scary, but simple. Hepzibah was waiting in the lobby with a suitcase, one of those big ones on wheels, you know, looking as if she was waiting for someone to pick her up. Only the suitcase was unzipped at the back, where she'd positioned it at the corner of the desk. That pretty much blocked the view, and Maggie had already told the little girl what to do."

"Nip inside and keep quiet." At the plain daring of the operation, Lobrutto looked admiring. "Lord, that took nerve."

"Yes, but once Hallie was inside, Hepzibah simply walked out to the parking lot, pulling the suitcase. She has a car of her own — they hopped in and presto, no one noticed a thing."

He frowned. "That still doesn't explain how you — "

Across the room McIntyre made his way through the crowd of children, crouching to admire a toy truck, then to sympathize over an elastic-wrapped pressure bandage. In moments he was surrounded. He caught her eye and waved helplessly.

She waved back and turned to Lobrutto. "How I knew it was Oliver and not Maggie? Well, by the tickets. They were lying on the bed in the hotel room."

McIntyre had reached the refreshment table and was making a hit with the pediatric nurses there, she noted with a twinge; just wait, she thought, until I get back on my feet.

"The tickets," Lobrutto prompted, "for goodness sake, what *about* the tickets?"

"What? Oh, yes — well. The thing is, you don't have to wait to get seat assignments at the boarding gate, you know — you can get them in advance. And naturally Maggie wouldn't want to be standing around in an airport. She'd want to board as quickly as possible, to get out of sight. So she had the seats assigned when she bought the tickets, and the assignments were printed on the ticket folders. Row 17, seats D and F."

She looked up. "Does that suggest anything to you?"

He frowned; then a look of enlightenment spread across his face. "Who's in the middle?"

"Precisely. If only Maggie and Hallie were meant to go, why not get the seats together? But if three were going, and of course the third would be Oliver — "

"Then where was the middle ticket?"

"Right again. That's when I was sure she meant him to run alone — which only made sense if he were the one most at risk. The one," she finished, "who'd done it. She wanted attention on herself just long enough so he could escape."

"Really." Lobrutto grinned distractedly, glancing at the stage. "Terrific. And now I really must — "

"Hey, Father," called the metal-armed boy, "come *on!*"

As Lobrutto hurried off, Edwina felt a hesitant touch on her arm and turned to find a child beside her chair.

"Hello," the little girl said gravely. She was about nine years old, with big brown eyes behind thick glasses. Her long dark braids were tied with red ribbons, and she wore a green turtleneck sweater, navy corduroys, and Buster Brown shoes.

"Hello, Hallie," Edwina said, holding out her hand. The child's fingers were icy cold. "Where's your mother?"

The child shrugged, her eyes not leaving Edwina's. "Over there with Mr. McIntyre. They said I should come and talk to you a minute."

"I see," said Edwina. "Are you enjoying the party?"

Hallie shook her head. "I want to go home. I'm glad my mom's OK, but I want my dad and I'm still scared."

Edwina nodded. "I guess this has all been very difficult for you. You must miss your dad a lot."

The little girl frowned at her thumb as if debating whether or not to pop it into her mouth. "I remember you. You were there when my mom got hurt."

"Right," said Edwina. "I was there, and I got hurt, too. Was there something you wanted to ask about that, or tell me?"

Hallie's head moved up and down. Tears leaked down her cheeks in two steady streams.

"I'm being good now," she managed, "in the day. I talk, and I don't suck my thumb, and I don't cry too much. I'm trying really *hard* you know, because if I'm good I can go stay with my grandparents in Vermont, maybe."

"Well, honey, if you try as hard as you can, I'm sure — "

"But then when I'm asleep it all gets canceled and I wake up screaming again. You can't pretend to be grown-up," she finished miserably, "when you're asleep."

"Uh-huh," Edwina said. "Yes, that would be a problem for you. Because the thing is you're not a grown-up, are you?"

Hallie looked startled. On stage, the actors began taking their places; around the room, nurses and aides guided children into small chairs.

"And even if you were," Edwina said, "sometimes grown-ups get scared, too."

"Oh." Hallie nodded slowly. "Were you scared?"

Edwina swallowed hard. The precise memory of how she had felt when she knew she'd been hit wasn't a bit easy to have, and it seized her in all its vividness now.

"Yes," she said firmly, "I was very scared. And sometimes I still wake up at night and it's as if it were all happening now instead of in the past."

Please let me be saying the right thing, she thought. Let me not be hurting her or scaring her, because for this you need a magic wand or at least a Ph.D. in child psychology and I don't have either one. Please let truth be OK for a nine-year-old.

"And then," the child prompted, "what do you do?"

"Then," Edwina replied, "I wait. I wait for it to go away, and it does."

"But," Hallie objected, "it always comes back."

"Yes. It does. We can't help having our feelings, and we can't help remembering them either. Still, that's not always bad — good feelings come back too, when we remember good things, don't they? In fact, you might try doing that on purpose — in with the good and out with the bad, you know."

"I suppose," Hallie said doubtfully.

Just then McIntyre reached Edwina's side, smelling of clean clothes and Old Spice aftershave. Behind him came Maggie with the young policeman, who was looking steadily more bemused.

258

"Refreshments," McIntyre said, "for the ladies."

"Thank you," Hallie said, accepting the offered cup and turning back to Edwina. "All right," she said, "I'll try remembering some good things. But you do it too, OK? If we both do it, it might work better. My dad . . ."

Her lip trembled; raising her chin, she began again. "My dad always says two heads are better than one, only not on the same body." Then she laughed, faintly but determinedly.

"Quiet, please," said one of the teenagers on the stage.

The play, a much-altered version of *Samson and Delilah*, was full of funny faces, pratfalls, and mock swordplay, its high point arriving when Delilah — Gina Krill, the girl with cystic fibrosis, Edwina realized, that's where I knew her from — snipped a bright pair of scissors very near the tall brown-haired boy's shaggy head.

Then abandoning her Samson for the moment she gnashed the scissors with wicked vigor directly at the audience, which oohed and ahhed gratifyingly in return. Even the littlest ones didn't seem a bit frightened, only wide-eyed with enjoyment.

"Uh-oh," McIntyre whispered. "That kid better watch out. She looks like she means business."

259

As if on cue, Jim Lobrutto took the boy's place. Edwina noted that for once the priest's expression looked legitimately prayerful and wondered what in the world he might be up to.

"I guess that red heart pinned to her toga is supposed to be her new one," McIntyre remarked, "right?"

Edwina turned, staring.

"From what I hear, that new transplant-surgeon fellow, Wilkins," he went on, "is supposed to be doing it. According to your Mrs. Friedlander, he's got his whole schedule practically set up already. And she — "

He angled his head at the girl now menacing her scissors over Lobrutto's scalp.

"She's his first customer."

Edwina stared. For a cystic fibrosis patient a new heart and lungs might mean years of life: two, or five — maybe even more.

"I am a substitute," announced Lobrutto in a deep, stagy voice; the children giggled nervously. Crossing his eyes, he got up and danced a little jig.

"A root-a-*toot* substitute," he sang, and he did the dance again, flapping his hands and slapping his sandaled feet.

The children quieted expectantly as he peered at them.

"And right now," Lobrutto intoned, "hidden in my hair is everything *bad* . . . and *naughty* . . ."

A chorus of oohs went round the room.

". . . and *sad*," he finished. "So — "

With an I-give-up gesture, he seated himself at center stage. Behind him the girl with the paper heart brandished her scissors, bright blades glinting in the stage lights; then she began cutting off his hair.

The children laughed, hesitantly at first and then in long whooping shouts as the priest's dark curls drifted down, baring first one side of his head, then the other.

At the back of the room the big doors opened and closed. Turning, Edwina glimpsed Tim Porter in his mailman suit, his arm curved supportingly around the frail form of Brady Williams. Behind them came Harry Lemon, his fierce protective glare softening as Porter lowered Williams to a chair, then bent to whisper solicitously and wait for the reply.

Williams grinned, eyes alight in a face that was like a skull. Porter laughed at whatever Williams had said. Standing over them Harry Lemon put a hand on each of their shoulders as if for support; then, shrugging like a man resigning himself to the inevitable, he began laughing, too.

"Look," breathed Hallie Dietz, "around his

head, where his hair was — do you see it? It's shining!"

But by the time Edwina turned back it was gone — if anything had ever been there. Only Lobrutto's human face shone from the stage, along with the faces of the others.

The boy with no hand. The girl with no breath. The man with no hair. And the rest: laughing, just for now.

Just for now, Edwina thought, feeling the child's small fingers curl trustingly in her own.

"I," said the little girl, "will remember this."